The QUEEN ALPHA:

The Tempest Series, Book One

Darlene Mellors

DORRANCE
PUBLISHING CO
EST. 1920
PITTSBURGH, PENNSYLVANIA 15238

Dorrance Publishing Co
585 Alpha Drive
Pittsburgh, PA 15238
Visit our website at *www.dorrancebookstore.com*

ISBN: 978-1-6853-7477-8
eISBN: 978-1-6853-7615-4

DEDICATION

So many people have inspired me to write, but a few stand out. They deserve a lot of credit for who I am today. My parents show me that true love takes hard work and commitment. People give up to easily these days. They have been married over fifty years and they love each other more every day. I love you Mom and Dad. My sons, Derek and Ty, the greatest gifts of my life have always been the two of you. I am blessed to be your mom. I am so proud of the men you have grown up to be. You are my heart. I love you both to the moon and back.

My best friends, Amanda and Steve, the two of you show me everyday that true friends exist. Both of you are my inspiration, my ride or die, and my siblings by choice. I don't think I would be the person I am today if I had not met you both. True friendship, love, and trust we have in each other. I appreciate and love you both! You both deserve to find your "fated mate."

Jason, the love of my life. After all the years we have shared, good and bad, we are an awesome team. My heart. My soul. Every day you show me the true meaning "fated-true mates." Thank you for your never-ending love, support, and belief in me. It means more than I can ever express. I love you.

I hope you all enjoy my version of true love. I loved doing it.

Thank You
Darlene

THE TEMPEST SERIES

PROLOGUE

As pups our parents told my siblings and me bedtime stories; I was always intrigued by a she-wolf named Zola. Every one thousand years the Moon Goddess would handpick a female wolf shifter to have the most power of wolves. She would be a pure white wolf, very beautiful and gifted with unique abilities that no other wolf shifter would possess. The powers she would possess were the ability to heal, telepathy, premonition, capable of white magic, heightened strength, speed, agility, lie detection, and being the fiercest of all wolves. She is the only wolf that the Alphas would bow down to. Her power surpasses everyone and would be known by all as the Queen Alpha, but with this gift comes a curse. The Queen Alpha would have one fated true mate. A fated true mated is her wolf's soulmate, other half, best friend and forever lover. This wolf is also handpicked by the Moon Goddess to be the Queen's perfect match. You are mated for life; when one dies, the other mate will die within hours. Connected to the soul. If a fated true mate rejects her, the Queen is destined to live out the rest of her life mateless, but if they claim each other by marking, they will become the most powerful couple in the world. They would be royalty, and so would their descendants.

My favorite is Zola's seventeenth birthday. Her and a group of friends went off to the lake to celebrate. As she got closer to the lake to celebrate, a smell consumed her. A smell of ocean and sand. As Zola look up, her world stopped. She was staring at the man she dreamed of since she was a pup; trying to catch her breath, she took him in. He was gorgeous, standing at six-four with the blackest hair and the bluest eyes. Like the ocean, she thought. He was talking and laughing with his friends. Zola just wanted to be near him. Finally, she got the courage to walk over and talk to him. Her wolf was yelling "mine" in her head; she felt the pull to him. As she stood by him, he didn't notice her. Zola decided to speak up and introduce herself to him. He turned to face her with an irritating look on his face.

"Hello, my name is Chance," as he extended his hand to shake hers. Zola felt like lightning just struck her. She dropped to her knees the jolt was so strong. When Zola looked up, she saw that Chance had a confused look on his face.

"Don't you feel that? You are my fated true mate. I feel it." Zola never looked away from Chance as she spoke.

Chance replied with a laugh, "What are you talking about? I could never be your fated true mate. I find you undesirable. I should find my mate attractive, and I don't." Zola was crushed. She asked the one question she feared the answer to.

"Do you reject—"

Before she could finish the sentence, Chance yelled, "Yes. Who would want you as a mate? What is your name?"

She responded, "Zola Westlyn."

The next words Chance spoke were the most heartbreaking "I, Chance Somerset, reject you, Zola Westlyn, as my mate." He did in front of everyone of her friends. Some laughed, while others were shocked. Zola took off running and sobbing trying to figure out why her mate rejected her.

When she reached a clearing away from everyone, she dropped to her knees with tears strolling down her cheeks. Zola looked up to the sky and asked the Moon Goddess, "Why did my mate reject me? Am I not good enough?"

The Moon Goddess replied, "You are enough, my child. I disguised your outer beauty to your mate. I wanted him to see that your true beauty lies within. I am sorry, Zola, that your mate was not the man I thought he would be."

"He rejected me! Will I live the rest of my life looking like this to him?" Zola asked.

The Moon Goddess quickly replied, "No, my child. Now that he rejected you, he will see your true beauty. If he would've accepted you, he would have seen it immediately, but he will never be with you. He was vain, and that action cannot go unpunished. I am sorry, Zola, but you will live the rest of your life unmated; you will have an accomplished life with love of family and friends, but not with a mate. This will be his biggest regret, for he will never be able to mate another. He will suffer the consequences of his actions as well."

Knowing that she would never have a mate crushed her. Trying to come to grips with everything that has happened, the Moon Goddess spoke to her one last time, "Zola, I know what you are feeling. I feel your pain and heartbreak. I vow today that your future generations will not suffer the way you are. In another one thousand years, I will bring a 'Queen Alpha' again, but this time I will bring help for her in the form of brains, brawn, beauty, and beasts. I shouldn't of put you through this pain to deal with by yourself. I will do better by you, my child. I am truly sorry. I love you, Zola, and I am here for you always!"

Zola felt the comfort that the Moon Goddess was giving her. She was looking out for her as she always did. After a while, she got up off her knees. She decided to walk back to the lake and try enjoy her birthday with her friends. Walking over to the big boulders next to the water and sat down. Pulling up her long, curly blond hair into a ponytail and watched everyone swim. After about ten minutes, Chance walked over to her and introduced himself to her. "You are the most beautiful woman I have ever seen. Your green eyes are exquisite." He smiled at her.

Zola stood up and replied, "I am Zola; you met me already. I know by the way you are looking at me right now that you know and feel that I am your fated true mate. I would have loved you with all my heart and soul. Because of your handling of my appearance earlier, I can see now that you're a shallow man. You don't deserve my heart." As she spoke, his jaw dropped in shock at her tone and fierce words. Zola continued, "Let me make this clear to you and everyone else here. I, Zola Westlyn, reject you, Chance Somerset, as my fated true mate." She jumped off the boulder and walked back to the pack she loved. Zola looked up to the sky and whispered, "Please, Moon Goddess, don't let another share my heartbreak. It is all that I ask of you."

ZOEY

As I walk into the packhouse heading to my office for an appointment, my secretary Quinn Ray yells, "Zoey, your dad wants you in his office ASAP!" Quinn is around my age, long, shoulder-length hair with brown eyes that match. She is a valuable asset to my practice. I look at her smile and roll my eyes. As I walk to the other side of the house, I can't help but laugh. I hate being called to my daddy's office. It's like being called to the principal's office; it is never good for me. As I open his office door, I see my daddy isn't here yet. I walk over to the big oak chair sitting in front of his desk and sit down. I look around to see all the pictures on the wall of our family and pack. It's what it is all about. My daddy, Zane Westlyn, is the Alpha of the Westlyn pack. Our pack is the largest pack in Pennsylvania. There are four packs that consume the state. The King pack is to the north, the Reese to the south, the Easton pack to the east; of course, our pack is Western Pennsylvania. We are all wolf shifters. Being a wolf shifter has its advantages; we are faster, stronger, smarter, have enhanced senses, live longer and heal quicker than normal humans. As I look at the pictures my daddy has on his desk, I smile. It's a picture of our family. My siblings Vixen, Melina, Zander and myself when we were pups. My daddy still thinks we are pups even though we are all in our forties. Then the picture of my mother Violet, our Luna. She is the heart and soul of our family and our pack. My mother is beautiful, with short brown hair, light green eyes, and is about five-five. It is funny watching her stand next to my daddy. They are a power couple. I admire them and the bond they share.

All of us pups went to college and got good educations. Three of us are doctors, and the other was a business major. My parents wanted us to succeed outside of the pack. I am a female Alpha, which is rare. I am the only one known in existence. My daddy wants me to take over as Alpha of our pack, but I am a psychologist and love helping people. It doesn't stop my Alpha from trying to guilt me into taking over.

I don't know how long I have been sitting here, but I have appointments. As I stand up to leave, the doorknob turns. I know it's my daddy. The door swings are open, and there is Daddy, all six-three of him with that mega smile on his face. I am blown away by how handsome he is for sixty-six-year-old man with bright green eyes and full head of silver hair. Of all my siblings, I am the one most like him.

"Good morning, Zoey! How are you today?" he asks.

"I am doing well, Daddy. Is something wrong? Did I do something I don't know about?" I tilt my head back to the side and smile right back at him.

"Not that I am aware of yet." He winks playfully.

I watch as he takes his seat behind his big mahogany desk. He props his feet up and leans back in his chair. "I have a decision I have to make, and I need your help to solve it." I sit up straight in my chair. I am all ears. He doesn't ask for help often, so it must be important.

"Okay, what is it?" It comes out in a high pitch.

He smiles and continues, "I knew you were going to say that. Got your attention. I need to tell you something important."

"Okay! Go ahead. I am truly interested," I reply.

"Over the past two years, the Reese pack has had some issues, and recently, Alpha Craig came to me to ask for help regarding the matter. He informed me that since his granddaughter Meadow was born, they haven't had a pup born. I mean not one. What is more perplexing is that no one has mated in that time frame as well. So, Craig asked me if I could send in a group of specialists to oversee the issue. We don't know if it's psychological or fertility issue. Since you are the best psychologist, I want you to head the team. Also, I want you ask your sister Melina to go with you. Melina is an OB/GYN and fertility specialist, so she will be intrigued by this. If you need to take Sasha with you, please do so.

What do you think, Zoey? Are you interested?" He watches me cautiously, waiting for my response.

As I sat there listening, I was intrigued as well. How does that happen? Why did it happen? Something didn't add up. I want to do it. "Zoey," my daddy said, "are you listening to me?"

"Yes, Alpha. I was just trying to wrap my head around the information you just threw at me. I will do it, but I need to talk to Melina, and Sasha to see if they are on board."

Daddy nods his head in agreement, but then his look changes as though he forgot something "Zoey, two more things before you leave. I know you have a busy schedule today. I remember the four of you are to go away this weekend out east, but I want this group out there in two days. I am sorry, but you'll have to cancel your trip, and the other thing, I know Sean hates being away from his sister since they only have each other now. Take him with you and he can work the numbers for me. Craig is going to pay for this." He winks at me. "He will have a cabin for all of you to stay together."

As soon as he said it, I was instantly mad. We have been planning this long weekend for months, but I understood this is important to my Alpha. On the bright side, we would all be together. "Call Alpha Craig. We will be there in two days, and I will go break the news to the gang about our 'no go' this weekend. Is that all you need from me, Alpha? I need to start getting my stuff in order and reschedule appointments before we leave." It comes out sarcastically.

"Zoey, I know you're mad at me, and I am sorry. You only call me Alpha when you're mad at me. But we must help them. If it was reversed, Craig would help us if we needed it. Craig and I have been friends since we were pups. He is worried, and quite frankly, so am I. It's urgent, sweetheart." I can tell by his tone he really is concerned. He has been a great Alpha his pack adores him. He is an even better dad. Over the years, he has kept some pretty big secrets for me and our family. Family and friends always come first.

I get up and go around his desk give him a kiss on the cheek. I whisper, "We will figure it out." I turn around to leave. Just like that I am hit with a severe headache that takes me to the ground. I haven't had one in such a long time. In a heartbeat my daddy is at my side.

"Are you okay? Have you been getting headaches again and not telling me?" His voice gentle but stern. "No, Dad, I am good. First one I have had in years. I will be fine, I promise." He helped me back to my feet and hugged me tight. I smiled and walked out the door. Once outside, I recalled what I saw. I don't want to see or feel it again.

As I walk over to the clinic, I am trying to decide how to break the news to my crew that our weekend away has been squashed by our Alpha. Walking in the door I see Sasha in her green scrubs. Sasha is five-nine with short, black hair, gray eyes, and the body of a super model. She didn't see how beautiful she really was. Grinning at me but then she notices I am not smiling back.

"What's wrong?" she asks

"We need to let our wolves out tonight to run. The four of us need to run and talk about the upcoming weekend. Can you let Melina and Sean know, please? I have to go to the office for a couple appointments. We can meet at the old oak tree at seven p.m., Okay?" She nods to my question and goes back to calling her next patient. I want to tell them all together. It's easier all at the same time.

As I was leaving, Melina called out my name, saying she needs to talk to me about something important. I make my way over to her. She starts to whisper. "Why are you whispering? I can barely hear you." She starts pointing at her ears and looks around the waiting room of patients. Melina takes me into another room and closes the door. She looks concerned.

"What's up?" I ask.

Then she starts, "Remember three years ago you donated your eggs to help that couple that was having trouble conceiving?" I nod yes. She continues, "Well, the woman that conceived a child with your eggs has requested today for us to do the procedure again."

I look at her. "They have a child and should be happy with that child. That is a secret you and I keep. No one but us is to know all of this. I just can't do it again, Mel."

"Well, it is odd when she called earlier; she sounded like she was demanding me to do it. She even volunteered to pay the donor whatever she asks for. Zoey, she sounded desperate." Melina looked at me anxious.

"I don't have time to deal with this right now. I have a lot on my plate. Can this wait?"

She nods yes. My sister is a beauty, standing five-six with long, curly brown hair to the middle of her back, beautiful sky blue eyes, and curves to die for. Although she thought she was fat, she wasn't. We are so opposites. I am five-three, long, blond hair and bright green eyes, but we share some of the same curves. "Mel, we are running tonight Old Oak at seven o'clock, you good?"

"Yes, I will be there, beffer." She laughed; she isn't just my sister, she is my best friend, so we make up crazy names for each other. I turn the knob, open the door, and walk out of the room with another bad feeling.

My day flew by fast. I rescheduled appointments and referred some of my patients to other psychologists. I don't know how long we are going to be away. As always, I am the first to arrive at the Old Oak; the other three are always late to everything. Sean arrived next; he is Sasha's baby brother about four years younger than her. Sasha and I have been close friends since we were pups, so Sean has become my little brother as well. He and my sister Melina are close in age and tight friends. Sean is the opposite of his sister. Standing six-two, broad build, blond hair, but Sasha and he shared the same deep gray eyes. I love Sean. He is a loyal friend, compassionate, a good man and sometimes quiet. Looking for his fated mate since he was young, he would talk about finding her one day. He will make a great mate. I really hope if any of us find our other half, it will be him. At 7:10, Melina and Sasha walk up to the old oak together.

"What's up, Zo?" Sasha's nickname for me since we were

pups.

I take a deep breath. "I wanted to tell you all together. We are going to have to cancel our long weekend." They look at me like they want to punch me.

Melina speaks first. "This better be good. We have been planning this forever. Why, sis? What is up?"

"The Alpha called me into the office earlier and enlightened me on a situation; he needs the four of us to go south to the Reese pack and address it. Apparently, they can't tell if the pack problem is psychological or infertility. Our weekend away is postponed, and we have to be there in two days. Alpha Craig is putting us up in a cabin on pack property. This conversation stays between us four; it's important. So, what do you all think?"

"We're in!" Melina and Sasha shout in sync.

Sean gives me a questionable look. "Why am I going? Not that I am disappointed to get away for a while."

"The Alpha wants you to keep track of the cost, but I believe he wants you to keep an eye on us three," I explain.

"I'm in as well," as he rolls his eyes at me. Knowing it's probably the latter.

"How long will we be there?" Melina inquires.

"As long as it takes to figure it out, I would image," I reply, hoping it won't take too long. Now that everyone is in agreement, it was time to let our wolves out to blow off the extra tension. We all take our clothes off to shift. Wolves don't have issues with nudity. It's normal for us to strip our clothes off at anytime to shift. My friends are breathtaking in wolf form. Sasha and Sean are gray wolves with those glistening gray eyes. Melina is a rare wolf. Her wolf is brilliant red with those big sky-blue eyes; she stands out in our pack. Then there is me; I am the rarest of all. My wolf is white as snow with luminous green eyes. There is no other female wolf like me. My friends think it's because I am a female Alpha, but I know the real reason.

For the next two hours we run, play, eat, and lie around in the grass relaxing. In two days, we are leaving and don't know when we will be able to be in our wolves again.

The next two days pass by so quickly. The van is loaded up and ready to go. My momma, the pack Luna, came to see us off and wish us well. She kisses us on the cheek and squeezes Melina and I tight. She keeps saying how much she will miss us. We jump into Mel's Mercedes-Benz Sprinter and wave goodbye! I will miss my boys and family a lot. As we pulled out, I lean my head on the passenger window and think back to the vision I had earlier. This isn't going to be easy to do. We are going into a pack to tell them that someone is trying to destroy them. I still don't have all the answers, but I know I need to find out.

COLT

My dad mind linked me early this morning wanting to see me right away in his office. I am sitting on his black leather couch unsure of why he went outside of our pack to deal with our pack issues. "I can't believe you told Alpha Zane about this. Why after all this time, Dad?" I am pissed at him right now.

"Son, it's been over two years, and Zane has specialists that deal with issues like these. We need answers. Our people can't find an answer. I must do whatever is necessary to help our pack. Do you understand how grave the situation must be for me to go to another Alpha for help?" Dad used his Alpha tone with me. "You are my oldest son and future Alpha of this pack. Right now, your daughter is the last pup born, and a lot of our pack members are questioning why."

"I know, Dad. I have heard all the rumors. Some say she is cursed. Other believe she is the devil and want her to die, believing it will make everything return to normal. I've heard it all. Tell me what you want me to do to make this better for Meadow. She is struggling with this as a child. No one talks to her or looks at her. Her own mother doesn't want to be around her. Please tell me what you need," I say, feeling useless.

I know my dad is doing what's best for everyone; he is a strong leader. Dad raised four pups, most of his life without his mate. I was four when my mom, Daisy, died giving birth to the triplets—Chase, Catie, and Cara. Growing up, our dad gave us everything he had, but he always felt guilty for not finding another mate. We knew our mother was not his fated mate. They were friends growing up. They fell in love and decided to mate, have a family, and prepare my dad to be the future Alpha. I still believe my dad is holding out for is fated mate. As I look at him staring out the window looking over the pack lands, he is in great shape for a sixty-six-year-old. He is muscular, midnight hair and eyes blue as the ocean. We all look like him. Alpha traits dominate. I hope my dad can find happiness one day, because he definitely deserves it. My dad starts talking again, taking me from my thoughts. "Colt, Alpha Zane is sending four people from his pack to oversee this situation. Two are doctors, a nurse, and I really don't know why the young man is coming. Maybe he is a mate to one of them. I want you to get your old cabin ready for them to stay in while they are here. Whatever they need make sure they have it at their disposal. Do you hear me, Colt? Colt, what is wrong?"

"Dad, I just don't need my secret coming out to these outsiders. I have kept this between you and me for twenty-four years!" I look at him feeling uneasy.

"Don't worry, son. No one will find out about that. It's been a long time, and no one has said anything by now. I am sure they won't find out," he reassured me.

"Okay! What time frame am I looking at?"

"Two days," Dad replied quickly. I stood up; I had to get moving, not much time to get the crew in there. I start to walk to the door. "See ya later. Have a good afternoon." He nods and goes back to looking out the window.

When I walk out of my dad's office, I see Stefanie Grant, the mother of my daughter, talking to an elderly woman. I have never seen this woman before, but they are having a deep conversation. She doesn't smell like a wolf. It looks serious for Stefanie not to notice or smell me standing here. As I approach them, Stefanie finally notices me. She moves the older woman with the shoulder-length gray hair to the elevator. Stefanie pushes the button to take the elevator to the first floor and whispers in the woman's ear, "Don't come here again. I will talk to you later." The woman nods, she keep her back to me so I never got a look at her face. Stefanie turns to walk to me as the doors close.

"Stef, who was that? You didn't want to introduce me to her?" She looks surprised by my questions—what is she hiding?

"No I didn't, Colt. She is one of my mom's friends from my old pack. She found out about me being with an Alpha and thought I could help her out financially. I told her I am not your mate yet. I explained I don't have that kind of money to help her." I knew this didn't add up, but I knew what was coming next out of her mouth. It's always the same thing. "So, when are you going to claim me as you mate and not just your baby momma," as she put her right hand on my chest, looking at me with desire. She was trying to distract me by trying to change the subject.

"I already told you, Stef, until this entire mess is resolved, we are not mating."

Then she came back with, "Is it because I am not your fated mate, Colt? Are you still holding onto hope she will find you after forty-four years of waiting? I thought you were finally going to accept us."

"No, Stefanie! I just have a lot going on and I am worried about our daughter. You do remember her? You don't spend any time with her. Now you want to mate and have another child. Why don't you pay attention to the one we have?" She has now pissed me off.

"I don't know, Colt. I just don't feel a connection to her. All my friends blame her for not being able to conceive or mate. And a part of me does as well. I am sorry, but it's true."

She is pushing my temper, and I yell in my Alpha voice, "You are her fucking mother! Who cares what others say! I have to go. I need to get away from you before I say something I'll regret. Good night, Stefanie."

As I leave, I start to make calls. First to my Beta, Diesel. I have him get the crew into my cabin to have it cleaned well. No one has been in it in years. Second to my Gamma, Ryker. I need him to train the warriors the next couple of days since I will be away on Pack Business. And lastly to my pack enforcer and Sheriff, Silver. He is going to make the drive with me to Philly early tomorrow morning. As I hang up, I need a drink and to relax, so I head over to The Queen Bar. It's close to the packhouse, and Millie, the bar owner, is a single wolf shifter in her late thirties. Her mate died five years ago from cancer. She decided to keep the bar and run it by herself. I am comfortable talking to her. She has a great sense of humor, and she pours my drinks nice and strong. She listens without passing judgement.

"How are you doing this evening, Colt?" as she pours my Tito's and cranberry.

"Okay, Millie! Busy! We have four visitors coming in tomorrow or the day after from the Westlyn pack to help figure out our pack problems. I hope they can fix it." I say it really believing that they can. Not just for our pack but for my beautiful daughter Meadow; she looks so much like me with that midnight black hair, but she has vibrant green eyes. I have no idea where they came from. Stef is a blond-haired, brown-eyed woman. She is pretty, but I just don't feel any desire for her. It made me feel like a horrible man, but that one-nightstand ended up producing Meadow. I love that little girl more than life itself. I just wish I didn't have to deal with her mother. We aren't compatible at all. One of the reasons I am a regular here is, so I don't have to deal with Stefanie. She would never come into this bar, so it is a safe place for me. I have tried over the past two and a half years to mate with her, but I can't bring myself to do it. Plus, I have a secret that I will never tell her. She will never understand why I did it. I try to keep her content because if she ever found out what I have done, she may take Meadow from me. So, I stay in this relationship out of fear. Stefanie was right earlier when she said about delaying the mating. She isn't my fated mate, and I still hoped that one day I would finally find her. The one the Moon Goddess made just for me. My one and only true love. That is what I wanted, I wanted that connection, the fire and the bond for life. As I sit here and drink by myself, trying to forget all my problems, just feeling sorry for myself, I realize 2:30 a.m. I have to get up in a couple hours to make a trip to Philly to pick up equipment for the new arrivals I need to help them in any way possible to find out what is happening so our pack can go back to normal and they can go back to where they belong without any more trouble. I get up and say good night to Millie. "I hope everything works out, Colt. Goodnight," she replies and goes to get another customer a beer.

ZOEY

As we pull into the Alpha's house, my wolf is on edge. This isn't like her to act like this. She is normally calm. As I get out of the van to walk to the packhouse, a man named Mason comes out to meet me. As he extends his hand to shake mine, I have another "headache," and my wolf growls. Something about him she does not like. Trying to gather myself together, I make up an excuse that it was a long car ride and I suffer from severe headaches. My wolf doesn't even like them, I explain. He smiles at me, but it's not genuine. He looks past me toward where the van is parked; I see something in his eyes. The way is looking in that area screams trouble. I am going to keep an eye on him. Mason leads me inside to Alpha Craig's office. I knock on the door, and he calls out to come in. As soon as I walk in, I feel a change come over me like I am home. It is very calming, and now my wolf is content. Thank the Moon Goddess. It is eerie how calm this place makes me feel. I haven't been here since I was fourteen years old. My dad and Alpha Craig have been friends since they were pups, and they trust each other completely. They all know most of my secrets and are all good Alphas.

"Zoey, I haven't seen you in a very long time. Your dad brags about you all the time. He said you grew up into a beautiful woman, but even your pictures don't do you justice. You are stunning," Alpha Craig expressed as he walks over to give me a big hug. "So, I hear my goddaughter has been doing really well for herself. I am sorry I haven't gotten to spend as much time with you in the last twenty years, Zoey. I miss our fishing trips at the Tempest every summer." He winks at me and smiles. "And call me Craig, not Alpha. You are a part of this family. Do you hear me?" I nod and smile back in response.

"Thank you, Craig."

"He brags about his three doctor daughters. Vixen and Melina being OBGYNs, and you a psychologist; he is so proud of all of you. Melina's specialty in fertility was why I called him and asked for a favor. So how are your boys, Derrick and Tyson, doing? They must be twenty-four and twenty by now?" I nod yes to the question, but he continues to speak, "I haven't seen them since we went fishing four years ago. Time really has flown bye. How are they?" he asks again.

"Derrick and his mate Erica are expecting their pup in two months. Our family is thrilled about the next Alpha; Derrick has done well for himself. He owns Mama Wolf Publications. My dad brags to everyone how his grandson started his own business and became a multi-millionaire at the age of twenty-three." I laugh, as does Craig. "Tyson will be defending his MMA championship in two months. My two Alphas have grown up since you've seen them. Tyson is so strong, muscular, and a formidable opponent to anyone. He is an overpowering six-three; the older he gets, the more he looks like me. Blond hair to his shoulders and piercing green eyes. Women love him, and he loves the ladies. Derrick, gorgeous with that short, coal black hair, a buff six-three, and eyes as blue as the ocean. Growing up, I called Derrick my brains and Tyson my brawn; it stuck with them as they got older." I laugh. "Sorry to go on and on about my boys, but I am so proud of their accomplishments. I'm a proud mom."

"You should be. Zane told me how you raised them by yourself. Zoey, that is amazing, and congratulations on your new addition. There is nothing like grandchildren. I love them." He winks at me.

"Thank you, Craig!" Happy to finally spend a little time with the man I looked up to as a little girl.

Craig opens the drawer to his desk and hands me the keys to the cabin we will call home for the foreseeable future. The directions are pretty easy that he gives me. We are close to the packhouse. Then he looks at me and with a seriousness to his tone says, "Thank you all for doing this for my pack; it means a lot to me." It's tough for Alphas to ask for help. I am really do everything in my power to help this pack. Craig also told me that he set up the second floor of the pack house with adjoining rooms, enough room for our medical machines and exam tables. He explained that "the machines will be here later this evening. My son, Colt, went to pick them yesterday." I acknowledge him, then I realize I didn't know how long I have been here, but my friends are waiting for me in the van. As I make my way to the door, Craig thanks me again for helping his pack. I smile, open the door, but as soon as I do I feel uneasy. All I can do is wonder, why this pack?

I get to the van and apologize for being so long, but apparently, I wasn't in the office as long as I thought. As we pull up to the cabin, we are all shocked by how gorgeous it is. Melina opens the front door; it is a modern ranch style. Four bedrooms, huge living room, three bathrooms, and the kitchen is gigantic. The kitchen is the heart of the home; in wolf shifter families, we tend to eat a lot. This is a place I could see myself living in.

"I love it!" Sasha yelled. "Zoey, you need to see the backyard!" I walked out onto the back porch. The view took my breath away. The lake was beautiful, a small beach and a pavilion with all the amenities. A large bar, wicker furniture, tables and chairs, refrigerator, and massive firepit. Whoever built this did an amazing job; they made it absolutely perfect. I am going to enjoy relaxing here when we are done working.

Since we aren't starting 'til tomorrow, we decide to jump in the van and get some groceries. On the way back from shopping, we see a bar, and Melina wants to stop. The Queen, I like the name. It's a small local bar, but I feel at home here. As we go inside and sit down at the bar, we introduce ourselves to the bartender, Millie. She is amazing. She is in her late thirties, chocolate hair, bright blue eyes, and curves most women would die for. She tells us about the events she has on Fridays and Saturdays. People are playing darts, listening to music, and just hanging out with friends. My kind of bar. This is a place I know we will be spending time in. After about an hour, we say our goodbyes to Millie, promising to come back Friday.

We are all up bright and early, having our morning coffee, getting ready to start our first day. When we get to the second floor of the packhouse, we find out the medical equipment we need isn't here yet. I need some fresh air, so I make my way outside. I am hit with another headache. The pain is so excruciating that my wolf is whimpering. I lean against the brick wall, waiting for it to subside. I haven't had one in three years. Why am I getting them so much lately? After it finally subsides, I look up and see my sister Melina talking to a little girl; she couldn't be more than two or three years old. As I walk over to the large stone bench where Melina and the little girl are sitting, laughing, Melina looks up. "Zoey, I want to introduce you to Alpha Craig's granddaughter, Meadow." When I get close to her, I find myself staring at her. Her bright green eyes, they look like my son Tyson's. She really resembles my boys. I must have been staring at her for a while because Meadow starts to talk drawing me from my thoughts.

Meadow says, "What's your name?"

"I'm Zoey, It's nice to meet you," as I kneel down to her height.

"You're pretty, Zoey."

I thanked her and told her she was beautiful as well. She blushes. She really is adorable. She went onto tell us about how pack members don't talk to her; she can speak well for a two and a half. Then it hits me. Her smell is different from other females. She is an Alpha female. I didn't realize that another existed. I will have to talk to Craig about it later. Just then, a big truck pulls in. Our equipment has finally arrived. When two guys get out, I stand up and yell, "It's about time!" They look at each other and laugh. The older guy turns and walks to the back of the truck to start unloading it.

Meadow yells, "Daddy!" takes off running to the driver of the truck.

Melina looks at me and laughs. "Smooth, Zoey." I turn red from embarrassment. I realize I just yelled at an Alpha. As he picks up Meadow and walks toward us, I smell the scent of ocean water and sand; it's the most amazing scent. I catch my breath. What is happening? I feel dizzy, and my heart is racing suddenly. The closer he gets to me, the scent is getting stronger. I can't stop staring him. He is tall, dark, and handsome. The shadow of a beard. Oh, Moon Goddess, he is gorgeous. Wow, I wish he could be my...

"Mate!" my wolf yells out. He is our mate! Look at that sexy hunk in front of us. I am overcome with emotions. I have never felt anything like this. My wolf is trying to come to the surface. It takes all my energy to not throw myself at him. My wolf wants to claim him as ours. She is excited to finally find out mate. I am trying to process everything. He is speaking to us as I am blocking her out. His voice is so deep, and it makes me feel calm and love all at once. "If you ladies need anything, let one of the guys know. They are taking your equipment to your rooms now. Have a wonderful day."

As he turns around with daughter in his arms, "What is your name?" I ask.

"I am sorry. I am Colt Reese, and what are your names?" he replies back.

"This is Melina, and I am Zoey. Do you know who I am?"

He looks at me and smiles. Oh boy! That smile. I am in love already. "Yes, I know who you are." I smiled at him. "Your Alpha Zane's daughters, and if I assume right, both of you are doctors. Also, Zoey, you are my dad's goddaughter." My smile fades. My mate does not recognize me. "Nice to meet you both." He turns and walks away.

Something is very wrong. I need to find out what is going on with this pack more than ever. My mate doesn't recognize me at all. But I know who he is. I look over at Melina, and she says, "What is wrong with you? You just turned white as snow. I have never seen you act like this before."

"Nothing," as I turn to walk into the packhouse. I am not saying anything to anyone until I know for sure what is going on here.

COLT

I am running late delivering this damn medical equipment. As I pull into the packhouse driveway, I see my beautiful little girl talking to two women I've never seen before. They must be from the Westlyn pack. Meadow looks so happy talking to both of them. I was taken aback when the one woman yelled at me as we got out of the truck. Silver mindlinks me, "I like her! She puts your Alpha ass in its place." Both of us laugh.

My wolf says, "She is an Alpha female." I am taken aback by that. I only know of one. I have to ask my dad about this later.

Then Meadow is running to me yelling, "Daddy!"

She backs down and blushes. Good! She knows who I am. As I approach her, I see a change in her body. Then she asks me my name. I really look at her. I can't help but stare at her bright green eyes. They are stunning. Just like my baby girl. "Colt Reese," I reply. "What are your names?" I ask to be polite. "This is Melina and I am Zoey." She stood confidently, looking at me. All I could do was stare thinking what a beautiful name for a stunning woman. Her eyes changed to an even brighter green when she looked at me and said, "Do you know who I am?" Well, she and her sister must be Alpha Zane's daughters and are doctors, I believe. She smiles at me. Wow, she is breathtaking. What the hell is wrong with me? I turn to the truck to Silver and the pack members getting the equipment out of the truck. I need to get out of here and get some sleep.

"Have a good day, ladies," I say, walking away carrying my girl.

Meadow looks at me and starts, "I like them, Daddy. They talk to me and make me laugh. I really like that Zoey. She says I am beautiful. Did you see her eyes are like mine, Daddy? Can I talk to them more?" She was so excited. All I could do is answer, "Yes, sweetheart!" I really like seeing her like this.

I left Meadow in her room with her nanny. Now I am on my way to my dad's office to deal with pack business. "It's about time you got here," Dad yells as I walk into the study.

"The equipment wasn't ready, and traffic was horrific, so we had to wait," I said in my Alpha tone.

"What's your problem, Colt? I was just messing around." He looks at me with smirk on his face.

"Dad, I just got yelled at by Alpha Zane's daughter for being late. I don't need to hear it from you as well."

He laughed. "She is a strong Alpha female, isn't she?"

Since he mentioned it, "I thought there was only one Alpha female. Why didn't I know about her?"

"Her dad, Zane, is one of my closest friends, as you know. He has tried to keep her a secret 'til she found her mate. Only the Alpha's family and close friends knew about her, and we promised him not to tell anyone. Alpha Zane would like her to take over as Alpha when he retires. Could you please try and get along with her since you are going to replace me? Son, you will have to deal with her a lot." He just smirked at me again.

"I thought he had a son to take over as Alpha."

My dad gave me a serious look. "Her brother is Zander Westlyn; he is the Alpha of the Easton pack. When Violet's father died, she was an only child. Zander was next in line to take over as Alpha."

"Now I understood the situation. Wait, did you just say she doesn't have a mate yet? How old is she?"

My dad comes back with, "Interested, son? I thought you have Stefanie." Now he's really laughing at me. My dad has never made it a secret of how he feels about Stefanie. "Well, you haven't found your fated mate either, son. Isn't she beautiful?" He is carefully watching me.

"She is beautiful, that is why I am shocked! Can we change the subject? I am starting to feel uncomfortable with this conversation." We move on to the pack business.

It's late afternoon and we are finishing up when there is a knock at the door. My dad yells to come in; there she is again. "Come and have a seat, Zoey." Dad points to the seat beside me.

"Thank you, Craig. We are finished for today," she says as she sits down. "I have something to ask you if you don't mind." She smiles.

"Go ahead, Zoey, ask anything. We will do anything to figure out what is happening to our pack." I noticed she kept starring at me the entire time my dad spoke.

"I have met with some members of your pack, and they have been very helpful. As you know, I am a psychologist, and my sister is a fertility specialist. We would like to sit down with each member to go over their medical history. Can each member make an appointment with each of us, please? I would also like to spend some time with Meadow and try—"

I cut her off talking about my daughter. "Why do you need to involve my daughter?" I growled at her.

She turned to me with anger in her eyes and growled back, "I am looking out for her." She used her Alpha tone on me. It doesn't work on another Alpha, sweetheart. "I want to make sure she is okay with the way people are treating her. I want her to understand this isn't her fault," she continued. "Listen, I think she is a smart, beautiful child, and I am here to help. I don't need you growling at me everytime I do or say something about her. I understand you're a protective dad, but I have two sons with grandpups on the way. I would never hurt a child." I am taken aback by the way she spoke to me. Most people cower to me. I am an Alpha, but then again, so is she. She is our equal, my wolf keeps reminding me. My dad brought me back to the conversation.

"Do you agree with that Colt?"

I just look over at her and say, "Yes!" I don't know what I just agreed too. We sit and listen to smaller issues, and Dad agrees to all her suggestions. She really is intelligent woman.

"Your dad must be very proud of you, Zoey." She smiled at me.

28

I was shocked by how good it felt to be on the receiving end of a smile instead of her temper. My wolf was laughing at the thought as well. "He is proud of all his children and grandchildren. I just happen to be the oldest and most like him. That is not always a good thing."

She grinned and then winked.

"Zoey, your dad informed me you will be taking over as Alpha when he decides to retire?" He had a look of concern on his face. What is he so worried about?

"He is pushing me to take over, but I just want to continue my practice and train our pack warriors. I am happy with doing that. He recruited you to help push me while I am here, I am guessing?" They both bust out laughing. I just sit here watching how these two get along. "Craig, my boys may come and see me if I am here for an extended time. Do I have your permission for them to enter your packlands?" The tone of her voice is so caring for her boys. She at least is giving my dad respect by asking for outsiders to enter our land. It's actually a law in our shifter community.

Dad answers immediately again. "I haven't seen them since Tyson's sixteenth birthday." He smiles at me like he knows I have a ton of questions to ask about this entire conversation. I do! She doesn't have a mate? She has boys with no mate? Female Alpha? Grandmother? This is too much. Zoey thanks my dad and stands to leave. We both stand as well. She shakes my hand, and I swear to see something change in her eyes. It is slight, but I saw it. She pulls her hand away immediately, like she is being burnt. Her scent changes as well. I could swear her wolf is coming to the surface. She walked over to my dad and gave him a hug. I felt jealous at that moment. I wanted a hug as well. What the hell is wrong with me? I need to get some sleep is the excuse I can come up with.

As Zoey is about to open the door, she turns around looks at my dad and winks. "Thank you, Godfather, for the cabin. It's beautiful. The view is breathtaking. The person who built it put their heart and soul into it. They did an amazing job. Please let them know from me. It is a place I would love to live."

Dad nods at her and she walks out the door. He looks at me. "Guess I don't have to tell you, you heard it for yourself." I smile at him with pride. I love that cabin. It took me five years to build it the way I wanted it. I built it for my mate and pups. Stefanie hates it, so we live in the packhouse. I yawn. "I am going upstairs to get some sleep; it's been a long two days." Walking to my room, I keep thinking about Zoey Westlyn; there is something about her that I really like.

ZOEY

As I walk to the cabin to grab something to eat, all I can think about is Colt. When I shook his hand, I felt like lightning struck me. His touch and scent kept drawing me to him. I had to pull it away fast before they noticed and started asking me questions; my wolf kept trying to take over, but I can't let that happen. She wants to claim him when he is around. I have so many questions. This situation just doesn't add up or make sense from a medical standpoint. Starting tomorrow, we will start getting answers. The pack members have appointments starting at eight a.m.

The next morning, I eat and make my way back to my temporary office, but I am not paying attention. I walk into a blond-haired, brown-eyed she-wolf. "Watch where you are going, bitch," she yells at me as she looks me in the eyes. Knowing this isn't my pack, I try to be respectful. "Sorry, my fault. I was in deep thought."

As I go to walk past her, she throws out. "You're that doctor, aren't you?" I nod my head yes. She has this penetrating gaze. Almost like she is looking into my soul. "Just stay away from my man and we will be just fine."

I, of course, respond, "Don't worry about that, I am sure he isn't my type anyway." She gives me an evil smirk, and as she goes to pass me, she shoulders me. I know she did it on purpose. This bitch was given her one and only time of me being nice; from now on she will get the Alpha female. I don't get intimidated by anyone. As I continue to walk to my office, I laugh to myself. I don't like that woman and I don't even know her name.

It's mid-morning and the pack members have been helpful with information. Most of the female wolves that I have talked to brought up Stefanie. Apparently, the woman I ran into earlier is Colt's baby momma. The only reason he stays with her is because of Meadow. He has had three years to claim her and still hasn't. Pack members gossip about how different she is with Colt than with pack members. She is fake. What a bitch. She wants the power of being the Luna. She doesn't even like her own daughter. She never spends any time with her. Many of the pack members believe Stefanie is the one saying all the awful things about Meadow. Something about this Stefanie just doesn't seem normal to me. A Luna is to be the heart of the pack, be loving and caring. Is she hiding things or secrets from the pack? Is she involved in whatever is going on? Maybe it's time to call in my pack enforcers for another point of view. I pick up the phone and make the call. After I hang up the phone with Nico and Jared, who are not only my best pack enforcers but two of my closest friends. Nico is what humans call a brother-in-law. He is my sister Vixen's mate. Jared and I have been friends since we were pups. He is also Derrick and Tyson's godfather. They are two wolves I trust completely. My enforcers will be here Monday or Tuesday to help me figure this situation out. After everything I have looked at today, it just didn't add up from a medical point of view.

It's Friday. I take a shower and get ready to go to The Queen for a couple drinks and clear my head from the day's events. I put on a pair of tight blue jeans, an off-the-shoulder green top, and a pair of black stiletto heels. When I walked out onto the porch, Sean, Sasha, and Melina are waiting for me. They give me a whistle. I blush. I know I look good. Sasha and Melina both have on black jeans with red dress shirts. Sean is in his typical jeans and black T-shirt. They look good. As I walk toward them I say, "Let's go get our drink on tonight!"

When we walk into the bar, his scent hit me. How can one person's scent impact me so much? Salt water and sand, my favorite place. The ocean makes me feel loved and secure. This is so new to me. I have always wanted to have a mate, and now that I know who he is, it hurts that doesn't feel the same for me. I look to the right; there he is, sitting at the bar. Millie was talking to

Colt and another big guy. Boy, they grow them bigger up in these mountains. They turn and look at us as we walk in. Millie winks at us. I really like her. She makes us feel so welcome. As she asks me what I would like, I order a Miller Lite and a shot of Kinky.

"Long day, sweetie?" she asks with a smile plastered on her face.

"A real long day," I reply with a wink and a big smile to match hers. We made our way over to a table. Sitting down, we start talking about all the inconsistencies of this fertility issues. Not coming to any conclusions, we decide no more business. "Shots! Shots! Shots!" I yell, trying to ignore Colt and that intoxicating scent.

"Let's play darts and sing karaoke," Sean says.

"Let's get drunk and have fun tonight. Tomorrow is Saturday, so we can sleep in," Sasha says, laughing. Melina got up first to sing Pat Benatar's "The Warrior." She is so talented in everything she does. Her voice is beautiful; when the song ends, she gets a standing ovation from everyone in the bar.

Sean leans into me and says, "Zoey, it's our turn." I look at him in shock. I know what we are singing. It's the song we sing together, "On Me" by Kane Brown. I love this song. It is about us. We will always have each other's back. It makes me happy to sing this with him. Just kicking backing having a great time with my friends. Soon as the song ends, the DJ says, "Zoey, stay here! You're up again!" I see the big guy that was sitting beside Colt walking toward me. I was going to sing a song with a guy I didn't know. With the alcohol kicking in, I thought, *Why the hell not?* Diesel is the guy's name. He doesn't say a word but smiles and looks toward Colt. As I look at Colt, I swear he looked pissed. His eyes were starting to change. Well, at least I have a reaction. Diesel looks amused. He is definitely playing with Colt. The DJ says we are singing "What Ifs," another Kane Brown song, which I love. We start to sing, and the place starts to sing along. Diesel has a really good voice. I had fun flirting with Diesel while we were singing. It made for a great show. I thank Diesel when the song ends. I catch Colt looking at me. His blue eyes are blazing. My body takes on a mind of its own when he is close to me. My wolf almost out of control to claim him. It took everything in me to hold her back. I realize he isn't looking at me but right behind me. There she is, Stefanie. I turn to see her, and I know my night is over. I can't be around her knowing she is with what is mine! I look over at Melina and mouth, "It's time to go." She nods. I walk over to Millie, give her a hug, and tell her we will be back soon.

She smiles and says, "I love having you and your friends here. A breath of fresh air. You all are always welcome here." I wave at everyone else, avoiding Colt's eyes, and walk out.

COLT

When Zoey walked into the bar with friends, I couldn't take my eyes off her. She looked so fucking hot. She may be the most beautiful women I have ever seen. Everyone here loves them especially Millie. They were having a good time together laughing and carrying on. Watching her singing with Diesel made me angry. I was going to walk over and talk to her, when I saw Stefanie standing behind Zoey drunk. Stefanie is wearing a black crop top with a black mini skirt. She looks like a whore. She looks like she is about to fall so I grab her by her by hips. Her hands touch my body and I feel nauseated. Her touch repulses me. Its why I still don't understand how we conceived Meadow. My thoughts go to my beautiful daughter and how I can't do this to her. Without another thought I pick up Stefanie and rush out of the bar. I am still confused why she showed up at the bar tonight. She never comes here. Why tonight? I am so pissed she came here tonight drunk. My night was ruined the minute I saw her. I take her back to her room in the packhouse. She passes out. Thank the Moon Goddess. I close the door and make my way across the hall to check on Meadow. My baby is sound asleep. I can't sleep; all I can think about is Zoey. Since she came here, I am consumed by her. Having weird feelings and emotions for her. I have never felt them before. It is bizarre how I love how her eyes look at me. I caught her multiple times doing it tonight. I love it more than I will admit to another person. I felt like an invisible rope was pulling me to her, but my wolf was silent. I lie on the couch in Meadow's room and finally fall into a deep sleep, thinking of those beautiful green eyes staring at me.

Zoey and I are naked in my bed in the cabin. Kissing Zoey, her kisses and touch are like fireworks on the Fourth of July. The way she kisses is so possessive. I love it. I hear her whimper as I groan. I want her like I could never get enough of her. She feels so good and so responsive to my touch. I look at her and whisper, "You don't want to play these games with me, Zoey."

She bites her lip and says, "I want to play games with you. Take me, Colt! Make me yours forever. Claim me! Mark me! I only want you, Colt!" I am lost in her…

"Daddy, wake up! You're talking in your sleep." Meadow is standing in front of me, laughing. So, I open my eyes and grab her by the waist and start tickling her. After about twenty minutes, I get Meadow dressed and send her to the kitchen to eat. My mind is starting to play tricks on me because I swear, she wants me as much as I want her. I think back to my dream; her kisses and touch were electric. I make my way to the shower, take my clothes off. I turn the ice-cold water on, but all I see is her. I take matters into my own hands and come while saying her name out loud. I lean against the shower wall, trying to figure out what is it about this woman that makes me want her and need her so much. She is making me crazy.

As I put on my jeans and black T-shirt, I remember I need to meet my dad in the office. I find myself hoping I run into Zoey. Just as I come around the corner, on my way to the kitchen, I see her sitting on the couch with Meadow as happy as ever. It makes my heart happy to see my baby girl overjoyed. This woman is even more perfect than I imagined. As I continue to watch them from the corner, I see Zoey put necklace on Meadow, then she lifts Meadow's chin up with her finger, so she is looking Zoey in the eyes.

Zoey says, "You are an Alpha female, never look down to anyone. You look them in the eyes. You are a lot like me. I will help you become stronger. No one will disrespect you while I am around. You and I are the only two Alpha females, we stick together." She calmly spoke to my daughter Meadow, hugged her, and Zoey kissed her forehead. It was emotional to watch; my little girl has found a hero. Zoey didn't see how amazing she truly was. I didn't want to interrupt them, so I went out the side door to the kitchen for my morning coffee.

As I enter the kitchen, I see Stefanie sitting at the table playing on her phone. She looks up and asks, "How is your day?" I tell her that I am extremely busy. It's a lie. It's funny that ever since Zoey came here, I realized more I really don't want to be around Stefanie. She bugs me about mating and having another child all the time. I don't want either with her. She stands up and walks over to me. Throws her arms around my waist and looks up at me. I know what this conversation is going to entail. We have had it a lot lately. "Colt, let's go upstairs and make love." She tries to be seducing but fails.

I look down at her and say, "I am not in the mood. We are not having another child. It will not make this relationship better. Do you even know where our daughter is?" She is taken aback by how direct I am being with her. I can tell by her facial expression that this isn't going to end well.

"She's upstairs with the nanny." She tries to pull me to her for a kiss.

In that moment, I hear a growl. I look to the kitchen door and see Zoey and Meadow standing there. What the hell was that for? Zoey looks at me, pissed. "Meadow is hungry. Can I get her something to eat?" As I step away from Stefanie, I get a feeling Zoey is upset with me, and I don't understand why. She barely knows me. I pick up Meadow and sit her at the table. I go to the cupboard grab a bowl and her Lucky Charms cereal. As Meadow is beginning to eat, I sit beside her, drinking my coffee. We are laughing and making faces at each other. Feeling someone looking at us, I look up to see Zoey watching us with a smile on her face.

"What?" I say to her.

She says, "My dad and I used to do this when I was younger and seeing you two like that makes me remember happy times from my childhood." Just then, Stefanie starts yelling about the necklace Meadow is wearing. I actually forgot she was in the room. Alpha tone comes out of Zoey.

"I gave her the necklace. Since her and I are the only two Alpha females, I gave her my necklace to boost her confidence. She is struggling; as her mother, shouldn't you know that already?" Then she tells, not asks, Stefanie that she has taken Meadow under her wing and will no longer accept any disrespect of this little girl. Including Stefanie. Stefanie is pissed and just leaves the room without saying another word. Meadow stops eating gets up and walks over to Zoey and hugs her tight. This little girl of mine has definitely found her new idol. Zoey hugs her back. I look at Zoey's eyes; they have gone black. It's like her wolf is taking over. Her and Meadow are hugging each other for a while. Zoey's eyes have returned to that brilliant green. She releases Meadow and whispers "thank you" to her. Meadow nods her head and returns to her chair to eat. As I watch these two, I swear that they are mindlinked to each other. That is impossible. Zoey isn't her mother or a member of this pack. Zoey looks at me like she knows what I am thinking and says, "Your daughter and I have a different bond. Being the only two Alpha females, it's a bond I just can't explain. Hope that makes sense, Colt." Her saying my name makes me unexpectedly happy. I just nod back to her sipping my coffee. Then Zoey stands up. "Have a nice day, and I'll see you later." I don't know which one of us she is speaking to, but I find myself hoping she was talking to me.

ZOEY

Leaving Colt and Meadow in the kitchen, I make my way to my office on a Saturday morning. I want to go over files from interviews I did yesterday. Someone knocks on the door. I already know by the scent who it is. "Come in, Colt," I yell.

He opens the door with a smile on his face. I try not to stare at him, but oh my goodness, is he hot. "What are you doing?" he asks

"Going over cases. Can I help you with something?" trying not to get aroused with him so close. As I stand up from my desk, I notice that he is staring right at my boobs. His eyes are starting to change. I quickly say "sorry," but my face is crimson red with embarrassment.

"Don't be, it's an amazing view." OMG! I am getting wet. He needs to stop talking.

Colt changes the subject. "There is a party at the bar tonight with karaoke again. It was a big hit last night, so Millie is doing it tonight."

"Thank you for letting me know. I will tell the rest of the crew when I get back to the cabin," I say, trying not to let off any scent of my arousal being around my mate is so incredibly tough.

"Thank you for everything you are doing with Meadow. I appreciate it. And hopefully I will see you tonight." He winks as he turns to leave. My panties disintegrated! I am so fucked by this situation. He has no idea what effect he has on me. Or does he?

As I walk into the cabin, the gang is sitting in the living room watching television. I inform them about the party at The Queen. Of course, they are in. I decide that I want to wear something a little sexy tonight. After my shower, Melina comes into my room to curl my hair and apply a little make-up. A short pair of black silk shorts, a silk, green spaghetti-strap shirt, and a pair of knee-high black boots is what I decide to wear. Taking one last glance at myself in the mirror, I smile, thinking I look hot. I am going to play with the man who doesn't know he is my mate. When I walk out of my room, Melina is the only one waiting for me. She looks beautiful in a pair of blue jeans and an off-the-shoulder purple shirt. Purple is her favorite color and she looks beautiful in the color. "The others are meeting us at the bar," smiling at me. I nod, and we walk out the door.

As we walk into The Queen, I am immediately hit with the scent of my mate. I look at the bar, and there he is, sitting with Diesel and another man. The other man looks a lot like Colt. Maybe his brother Chase. I haven't seen him since I was a pup. They stop talking to each other and turn to look at us. I swear I hear growling and laughter coming from them. We head to the table that Sasha and Sean are already sitting at, Sean stands and says, "I got the first round." He starts to walk over to Colt, Diesel, and the other guy. Sean is talking to the guys, and Melina walks over and starts taking the drinks from Sean, bringing them to Sasha and I. She looks mad. "What? I am thirsty and he isn't moving fast enough for me." She is turning red as she looks over at the bar.

"Melina, who is the guy with Colt and Diesel?" I ask.

"Chase the douchebag," she growls out. Sean comes back with a tray of eight shots and interrupts our conversation.

What is wrong with Melina? She is acting different.

"Let's have fun tonight since we were interrupted last night," Sean yells over the music.

"Let's show this pack how to party," Sasha says as she throws back her first shot.

Sasha is the first one up for karaoke. As she walks over to the microphone, I notice the classic black dress with black flats she is wearing. She really looks like a supermodel. My friend is stunning in whatever she wears. I wish she could see how beautiful she is. As she beings singing her favorite song, "Raise Your Glass" by

Pink, I see her smiling and moving around. She is having a good time. Sasha is a really gifted singer. She has a raspiness to her voice you don't hear too often. She rocked the song.

Melina is called up next. I watch as she whispers into the DJ's ear and turns to me, and I see sadness in her eyes. The song begins, and I hear a song that she has never sang before. Melina always picks songs that mean something to her. I listen closely to the words—"Want Me Back" by Lindsay Ell—Wow! She is good! If this artist sings this song with as much emotion as Melina, I may have a new artist to listen too. Something catches my eye from the bar, and I see Chase staring at Melina. A little smirk is on his face, and I swear I heard a growl. Turning back to Melina, she is staring daggers at Chase. This is interesting. When Melina finishes, everyone is whistling, screaming, and clapping for her. As she returns to the table, I say, "I never heard that song before. You were amazing!"

"Thanks, it's something different from my normal oldies stuff I normally do." Her tone is off. I hug her.

I whisper in her ear, "What's going on with you and Chase?"

Looking me in the eyes, "Nothing! Drop it, please! I don't want to talk about him. He doesn't deserve my time. Let's have fun tonight." I say okay, but I notice she is looking right at Chase's backside. Looking back and forth at the two of them try to piece together what the hell is going. The DJ interrupts my thoughts by calling my name to come up and sing. My friends put a song in for me because I fucking didn't. I look over at them, and they are all laughing at me. Raising their glasses at me, yelling cheers! What have they done? This is going to be embarrassing.

The DJ smiles and announces, "We have a two-song request for this young lady."

I point at myself and laugh. "Young lady, me?" Well, he is about my parents' age, so I guess I am young compared to him. First song is "Come and Get It" by Selena Gomez. I am going to kill these three when I am done. I am blushing red as a turkey-cock. Assholes!

COLT

As I sit at the end of the bar watching Zoey sing that song, I swear she is looking at me. The way she is moving around singing to all the people in the bar. She is giving one hell of a performance. Hot as fuck! I can't keep my eyes off her. Then Chase is acting so weird sitting next to me, and Diesel is laughing his ass off at both of us. When Melina was singing, I swear I heard him growling. What the hell is wrong with us since these four came here? I am having dreams about a woman I shouldn't. I am drawn from my thoughts when the old fucking DJ smiles at Zoey and says, "That was amazing. I can't wait to hear your next song. You have the voice of an angel." Is he fucking hitting on her? He is old enough to be her dad. Then it hits me. I am fucking jealous.

Zoey is about to sing her second song. She looks over at her friends, mouthing "assholes" at them. It brings a smile to my face. They have a close friendship. Zoey is an amazing person; it doesn't surprise me that everyone loves her. When the music starts, she closes her eyes and starts to sing. I have heard this song on the radio lately. It is a good song but hearing her sing it I swear she is singing it to me. Her voice does something to me I can't explain. "The kind when you don't look one." She opens her eyes and looks right at me. Her eyes are glowing bright green. I am blown away by the beauty of her eyes. The way she says "he's all mine" makes my wolf happy. Turning on my stool, I have to put my back to her; my wolf is getting aroused. He needs to calm down. The song is finally over. I hear people screaming and applauding. Turning around, I see everyone standing and I am so proud of her. She bows with a huge smile on her face, walking straight over to her friends she punches Sean in the arm. He is laughing so hard he has tears rolling down his cheeks. Zoey sits down looks right over to me with a big smile, then winks. A feeling stirs within me, and I smile back. I can't describe what her winking made me feel, horny. She looks so beautiful with that smile on her face. I would do anything to keep it there. I turn back to my drink, and I catch Chase staring at me.

"What?" I let out a sigh and take a gulp of my drink.

He grins at me and says, "What is it about those four?" He gestures his head toward Zoey's table.

"I know. I was thinking the same thing," as I look at him in agreement.

It's getting late and I need to head home. Millie takes my money for my tab for the evening. When she returns with my change, she mentions, "Best thing that has happened to us in a long time." She points right at their table and continues, "They have been a ray of sunshine to this pack. Something we haven't had in a while. I really like them."

Handing her a tip I say, "Yes." Heading onto my truck, I don't look at her. My head has been screwed up since she came here.

"Your mine!" She is taking off her green silk shirt.

"Yes!" I reply. The look in her eyes tells me she is desperate and needy for me. "Please, Colt, I want you to be my first." I like it when she begs me. I walk over to the bed and sit on the edge. She follows me and stands in front of me, topless. I lean forward and take her nipple into my mouth, sucking and pulling that makes her shake. All I can smell is her arousal. It is so strong. Feeling her need to be filled by me. My wolf was coming to the surface wanting to claim and mate her. She whimpers. "Colt, you're mine! Please claim me. I never wanted anything more than this. I have saved myself for you." Needing to feel her skin on skin, I start taking off my shirt.

"Daddy! Daddy!" Meadow is standing at the foot of my bed crying. Crawling down to the bottom, I grab her and bring her to lay beside me. I look down at her. Tears still running down her cheeks, but her eyes are closed, holding her teddy bear close. Meadow doesn't say another word, but I know she is having bad dreams. Although, she will never tell what they are about. Now that I am awake, I lie there for hours thinking about the woman who is consuming my every thought, awake and asleep. What is it about Zoey Westlyn that makes me want her so intensely?

Apparently at some point I fell asleep, because when I wake up, Meadow is gone. I get a cold shower and throw on a pair of jeans and an old, grey T-shirt. I head to the kitchen for coffee before heading to the office. As I round the corner, I hear a beautiful sound. My little girl is sitting at the table, still in her pajamas, laughing. I look to see why she's giggling. Zoey! She is the reason Meadow is happy. They both stop laughing and look up at me standing in the entryway. "Daddy, is it okay to go with Zoey today to the cabin and swim at the lake? Please, Daddy!" she asks excitedly.

As I make my way to the table and sit next to Zoey, I look at her and say, "Do you have time for that?" It came out a little sharp. I didn't intend it to, but I am on edge around her. When she looks at me with those fucking eyes.

"I always have time for Meadow." The way she responds it makes me feel lousy for being harsh to her. She is one of few people who want to spend time with Meadow. I look at Meadow and realize the situation of eating breakfast together seems normal.

Looking over at Zoey, I lean over to her and whisper, "Sorry, I am not used to this. Most people avoid her. Meadow can go with you today, and I will pick her up when I am done working." Goddess, being this close to her, I would love to kiss those lips and taste her. I immediately sit back in my chair, needing space.

She nods in an agreement with me, then turns to Meadow and speaks, "Let's get you upstairs and pack a bag for today." Meadow is already out of her chair and on her way up the stairs to her room. She is excited. Zoey gives me a smirk and waves goodbye, following Meadow up the stairs. I finally relax by myself and drink my coffee.

After breakfast I head to the office. Dad is already sitting at the desk doing paperwork. I sit down in the chair in front of his desk. He looks up at me. "What's up, Colt? You look like something is bothering you." I need to talk to someone; it might as well be my dad.

"Dad, I have been having dreams about a she-wolf lately. She is consuming my every thought. I don't understand any of this. What is it about her that I find myself wanting to spend time with her and I love being around her? What do you think is wrong with me? I am with Stefanie. I shouldn't be dreaming about another woman." As I finish the sentence, he is grinning at me.

"This is about Zoey, isn't it?"

I nod, and he continues, "She is a special one of a kind she-wolf. What you are feeling sounds like the mate pull. Are you sure she isn't your mate?"

"No, Dad, my wolf has never recognized her as our mate. Although, I would love it to be her. She is amazing, beautiful, smart, loving, and hot as hell. But with mates, you know that we know from the moment we see or smell them they are our other half. They need to claim and mark them, so every other wolf knows that they are ours for life. I don't feel that coming from my wolf. He just gets horny."

The way dad's facial expression is right now means he is concerned. He stands up and walks around his desk, standing in front of me; he opens his mouth. "Being an Alpha is tough, son, especially when you don't have your Luna, we crave her. She completes us. Then on top of that, you are worried about Meadow. Stefanie is no help to you. She adds more stress with mating and producing another child. Our pack is suffering right now. I don't believe this has anything to do with my granddaughter. Someone is putting that into our pack members' heads. I am starting to believe that what is going on isn't medical and bigger than anything we could fathom. That being said, do you think that the issues with the pack might include you as well? I am just talking to you as your father, not your Alpha. You take or leave my advice, but it's your choice." Sitting here listening and comprehending everything he's told me, I begin to think he may be right. What if this entire situation is more than a medical problem. But what? Then I hear my wolf say something that I never thought of. What if it is... Magical! Fuck, this could be worse than any of us imagined.

ZOEY

Walking out of the back house with Meadow, I pull out my phone out of my pocket of my jogging pants and call Melina. She answers on the third rang. "Hey, sis, I was thinking of going to the beach today and get some sun. Try and relax. What do you think?"

Melina's voice is raspy, and I know I just woke her up. "Zoey, sure, but I am still in bed. Give me at least an hour. It is Sunday, and I finally get to sleep, and we have been working a lot the past couple of days."

"Okay, I also need to run something by you! Meadow and I will see you soon." We make it to the cabin, and we both change into our bathing suits. Mine is a simple two-piece green bikini, and Meadow has a cute one-piece *Paw Patrol* suit. I pack a bag with tanning lotion, towels, and water as we wait for Melina to finish getting ready.

Lying on the beach, it is exactly what I needed to clear my head. Watching Meadow making sandcastles by the glistening water on this beautiful eighty-four-degree day. Feeling the sun kiss my skin always helps me relax. I am trying to figure out how I discuss this with Melina.

Melina looks at me. "I know you have something on your mind. Just tell me what's going on in your head, Zoey!"

As I turn over onto my stomach, I whisper, "What I am thinking can't be possible, but it is all I can come up with. Even my wolf keeps saying it."

"Tell me, Zoey! You know you can trust me," Melina whispers back so Meadow doesn't hear us.

"It's crazy, but I feel this connection with Meadow." We both look over at her playing in the sand. I continue, "I believe Meadow is my daughter. Melina's eyes look like bug eyes. She is shocked by what I am saying. "

"Zoey, do you know, or are you guessing? Because I know you are usually right when you see what is going on." Melina knows everything about who I am and how my headaches tell me things. She is holding her stare, waiting for my answer.

I look at her all serious. "Mel, can you run a DNA test on all three of the kids? I believe that Colt may be the boys' father. Top secret!"

She nervous but says, "Zoey, you know what that means, don't you?"

"I do," I reply. I change the subject to the Alpha and his Luna that want my eggs for another child. "Melina, investigate this further, because it just doesn't add up for me. It isn't sitting right. Also, I want you to go back to our pack to do the DNA tests. What I am going to say sounds unbelievable, but I don't think this pack situation is medical. I truly believe it is magical."

Melina agrees. she says, "After everything we have done the last couple of days, I believe you may be right. After all the tests we ran, none of these females are sterile. They should be having pups. It just isn't adding up from a medical standpoint." Melina is leaving for our pack tomorrow morning. Now that I have voiced my concerns to her, I want to rest for the remainder of the day.

We get back to the cabin, we all shower and change. I get Meadow a peanut butter and jelly sandwich. Looking at her eat, I think about the connection I have with this two-year-old little girl. It was strange, when I had my headache earlier, she touched me, and the pain disappeared. It was like she knew how to help me. What I saw has given me some answers but leaving me with more questions.

Around four o'clock, Colt shows up to pick up Meadow. He walks up to the pavilion where we are sitting and talking. He has on a pair of gray sweatpants and a black muscle shirt. Fuck, he looks so hot and sexy. His hair is still wet from the shower; he must've taken before coming here. We are staring at each other.

His scent is driving my wolf crazy. "Mine!" she keeps reminding me, like I don't already know. I realized I missed being around him today. Meadow is the first to speak.

"Daddy, can we stay for dinner? I like staying with Zoey."

Colt smiles in her, then leans down and kisses her for head. "No, sweetie, we have dinner with Grandpap every Sunday. We don't want Grandpap to be upset. Maybe another day, okay?"

She smiles back at him and says, "Okay, Daddy!"

He stands up and takes Meadow's hand. "Tell Zoey goodbye! And thank you, Zoey, for spending time with her today. I appreciate it." Something is different in his eyes when he was speaking to me.

"You're welcome! Anytime! I really enjoy spending time with her," I say as I walk over and give Meadow a hug. They start to walk away, but Meadow turns around and waves at me. I blow her a kiss.

When I look up, I see Colt looking at me. OMG! I want to feel him, taste him, all of him right now. "Goodnight, Zoey!" They turn and leave. I stand and watch them until they are out of sight. I miss them both already.

After dinner, I go out to sit at the firepit, drinking a glass of Moscato wine. Sean and Sasha join me. I realize as we are sitting out here together that Sasha hasn't been around much. She disappears when she isn't working. Sean has been working with the pack accountants, for the Reese pack because money is being lost with all the issues they are dealing with. He is great with numbers. Even though we joke around saying he came along to keep an eye on us, he really is trying to help this pack conserve money during this crisis. I am glad he is here with us. We love picking on each other, so I find an opportunity to pick on Sasha. "So, Sasha, what have you been up to lately? We haven't seen much of you around the cabin," I blurt out.

She won't look at me, but her cheeks turned bright red.

Sean, of course, chimes in, "Well, sis, are you going to tell us? Inquiring minds want to know." We both laugh at her expense. I know she isn't ready to tell us her secret, but it doesn't mean we won't keep asking. We sit for a while longer talking about work and the kids. Soon it's time to head to bed. We say our good-nights.

Waking up this morning, I have a strong urge to see Meadow. I miss her. Maybe I will take her for a walk in the woods. Since work is meaningless, my wolf and I would like to spend more time with her. Walking up the stairs to her room, I hear arguing voices. I walked past, trying to eavesdrop, but they are so loud it can't be missed. It's Stefanie yelling at Colt about how he is out every night and doesn't come home until she is asleep. She starts begging him to mate her. Then she starts about how she wants another child. Then he uses his Alpha voice; it's intimidating, "It will never happen. You don't even spend time with the child you have. I am tired of having the same argument all the time. Then he says the one thing to really piss her off, "You know, it's funny, our daughter lights up and wants to spend time with another woman. She talks about her all the time."

"I know you're talking about that great Zoey," she is scream-ing but continues. "Everyone thinks she's special. I think she is fake." I almost burst into the room, but it's not my place or my fight. I turn and walk to Meadow's room. She doesn't need to hear any of this; she is an innocent child. I knock on her door and walk to her room. Meadow is sitting on her bed crying.

"What is wrong, princess?" I calmly say, walking over to sit beside her on her bed.

"They are fighting again. She doesn't like me, Zoey. My mommy doesn't like me."

I pull her into a hug trying to calm her. "Your mommy loves you more than anything! Trust me!" I feel it. The pull to her. I am her mommy. Melina should be back late tonight or tomorrow with the answers they need. I look into her green eyes and ask, "Do you want to go for a walk, princess?" I put her shoes on, and we leave her room, walking toward the back staircase so she doesn't have to listen to them arguing anymore. "Protect her!" my wolf keeps telling me.

We are walking in the woods for about ten minutes in silence when Meadow stops and looks up at me. "Zoey, can I see you wolf?" This little girl has been through so much today, so I agree to let my wolf out. My wolf is kind of excited to meet Meadow. I walk around a big oak tree and take off my clothes. I shift. When I step out from behind the tree, Meadow is excited. Dropping to her knees in front of me, she brings her right hand up to pet my fur. So I lick her. She is laughing. "You're a beautiful wolf. I hope my wolf looks like you. I have never seen an all-white wolf before." My wolf is happy she likes us. I walk back to the tree to shift back and redress. I hear a sound of bones cracking. I quickly turn around to see a little white wolf with two black front paws, standing in Meadow's place. She walks over to me, starting to rub up against me. I drop to my knees and bring her close to me while petting her. That is when it hits me. She really is my daughter. A young wolfs first shift is either with its Alpha or her mother. Craig is her Alpha. She starts to run around, and I just want to be with her to celebrate this milestone. I shift back to my wolf. We run, roll around, and stay in our wolf form. I am honored that I got to see her wolf first. Bonding with my daughter after two hours, we shift back into our human form. I remember she tore her clothes on her spontaneous shift. I put my clothes back on, wrap her around me, and run to the pack house. We make it to her room unseen. We don't say a word to each other until she is dressed and sitting on her bed. Meadow looks up at me and calmly asks, "Are you my mommy? I felt like you were my mommy. My wolf kept saying, 'Shift for our mommy.'" As she is talking, I have tears of joy running down my face. I nod yes because I am too emotional to speak. My little princess jumps into my arms, squeezing me around my neck. When she pulls away, she has a huge smile on her face and says, "I can't wait to tell Daddy."

I freeze. "Meadow, we can't tell Daddy yet. We need figure out how and why this happened. And we don't Stefanie to find out either. Can we keep this a secret between us for a little while, please?" hating to keep another secret from the people I love.

"Yes, Mommy! I will do anything for you," she replies, looking at me with those beautiful green eyes. My eyes.

"Say it again, Meadow."

She gives me a questioning look, then she smiles at me and says, "Mommy!"

I am overjoyed. "I love you, my beautiful princess Meadow. Now I need you to lie down in bed and take a nap. Your first shift usually makes us tired. The more you shift, the easier it will become." Lying beside my daughter as she falls asleep is overwhelming. Once she is asleep, I kiss her on the forehead, whisper in her ear I love her, and cover her up. My daughter will never again question how much she is loved.

Descending the staircase, I see Stefanie standing at the bottom with her hands in her pants pockets. "I have been looking for you," she says, then continues, "Zoey, can we talk in Craig's office, please?" I nod and follow her. It's time to get the answers to my questions. I believe she is the only person that can answer them. As we enter the office, she sits on a long brown leather couch. I sit on the twin couch across from her. She sits staring at me, saying nothing. What is going on in her head? She wanted to talk. Finally, after a few minutes, she stands, walks over to get a bottle of water. She asks if I wanted one. I say yes. She hands me the water and sits back down in the same place she was before. As I take a sip of my water, she says, "Your friends and you need to leave here ASAP!"

Smiling at her, "We aren't going anyway. I may never leave. It's beautiful here."

Her look changed, and she comes back at me with "I know your secret, Zoey."

"I know yours as well, Stefanie. You don't scare me." Suddenly, I feel funny. "Stefanie, what did you do to me?" I growl.

She is laughing, "I drugged your water, you bitch." I am dizzy. The room is spinning. What is happening to me? Before I can do anything, darkness consumes me.

ZOEY

Waking up in a pitch black, cold cave. I try to remember what happen to get me here. I was in Craig's office talking to Stefanie when she said she drugged my water. I know she used wolfsbane. It makes wolves weak. The dose must have been strong to knock me out. Someone is entering the cave. There are lit torches hanging on the wall. That is when I notice that I am in a cell with silver bars. The shadow of the person is walking closer to my cell. Lying on the cot, I try to lie still because I need to conserve my strength. Then a scent hits me, but it's off. It's Jared! My enforcer and close friend. Why is he here? Did he do this to me?

He starts talking. "How could you do this to us?"

"Do what?" I haven't talked to him in a couple days. Finally after a couple minutes, I reply, "I don't know what you're talking about, Jared."

He walks closer to my cell and shouts, "Stop lying for a change, Zoey! You knew that he was your fated mate and didn't think we should know. You could have told me." I am in openmouth shock. I can't believe he knows. I made sure that on one besides Melina knew that Colt is my true fated mate.

"How do you know?" I look at him and calmly talk to him. I see the hurt in his eyes. Something is different with him.

"She knew that you were his mate, and when she told me, I didn't believe her. You would tell me everything. Why, Zoey? Why didn't you tell me?" He is hurt and pissed at me. I feel it all coming from him.

"Jared, who is she? Who knows this? I didn't want anyone to know anything because of what is going on with this pack. I didn't want to put anyone in danger. As my friend, I thought you would understand that. Did you put me in here? Are you helping this woman?" My voice is starting to use Alpha tone.

He looks at me and yells, "Shut up, Zoey! You were to be with me. I thought we would be together after all these years. Neither of us found our mates, so I believed you would eventually be mine."

I sit up on my cot and look him in his brown eyes. They look blacker. Screaming back at him, "What the fuck is wrong with you, Jared? This is not you talking to me. We have had this conversation many times over the years. We both knew our mates were out there, so we decided to wait for them." I am totally thrown off by him saying this. It really isn't like him. "Who are you helping? What is wrong with you? You know I love you like my brother. I have never given you reason to believe otherwise. My boys look at you as their uncle. They are going worry about me. They are protective of me." I start crying, thinking of someone hurting my children.

"Please, Jared, talk to me," calmly speaking to him.

By his facial expressions, he is fighting a battle inside his head. "Stop it, Zoey!" he growls at me. "Stop trying to get in my head. Is it true? Is he your fated mate? You owe me the truth. If you value your life, you will tell me the truth."

Looking him in the eyes, I say, "Yes, he is my true fated mate, but he doesn't recognize me as his mate. That is the reason I haven't told anyone. So, I want to know who this woman is who knows. Why are you my enemy suddenly?"

"I am not your enemy, Zoey," he says in a caring tone. He continues, "The boys aren't looking for you. No one is coming for you. They all think that you left for the Tempest for a couple days to relax."

"Why would they think that, Jared? They will never believe I would go there alone." I am so pissed off I can't help but scream. I need to get out of here. Then another scent of another entering the cave. The smell is making my head hurt. I feel sick. It's an old woman with shoulder-length grey hair and rare amber eyes. She isn't a wolf, but she is supernatural. Fuck, she is a witch.

"Oh, don't try and mindlink anyone. With the wolfbane in your system from the water you drank earlier and in combination of the spell I put on this cave, no one will hear you."

Looking at her, it hits me she cast a spell on Jared as well. "Who are you? Why are you doing this to me?" I question her.

She replies quickly, "My name is Jarrah, and I know you know I am a witch. Yes, I was told to put a spell on your boy here to help her kidnap you and bring you here until she decides what she is going to do with you." She sounds disgusted by what she is doing to me. Jared looks at her and smiles.

"She thinks they are going to look for her. We know that isn't going to happen." As soon as finishes the sentence, I fall to the ground with the worst headache I have ever had. That's when I see everything and let it consume me. I don't want to fight it anymore. I have no idea how much time has passed, but when I open my eyes, the witch is inside my cell with a bottle of water. I don't take it. I can't take the chance that is has more wolfsbane.

Grabbing her hand, she drops the water. I whisper, "Why?" Still weak, I don't have the strength to fight yet. My wolf is trying to heal as fast as she can.

Jarrah whispers back, "I am sorry. I have to do this." Her amber eyes are looking sadly at me. I know she means what she is saying. Confused, I let go of her. I lie back down on the cot, trying to make sense of the situation. I close my eyes and rest. I need my strength.

When I wake up, it's dark outside. Jared and Jarrah are no longer in the cave. I lie on the cot thinking about the vision earlier. My memory goes back to when I was sixteen years old....

Just finish training with my close friends Nico and Jared. Nico and I fighting about what an asshole he was during training. The first horrific headache I ever had took me to the ground. Grabbing my head and screaming. Nico blamed himself, believing it was his fault. It had nothing to do with him. That was the day I knew I had come into some of my powers. The day my visions, premonition, would tell what the future would hold for me and the people I love. They told me to talk to my Alpha's mate. We did everything together! We trained hard together. They made me the pack warrior I am today, and I made them the pack enforcers they are. On that day, I knew in my visions that neither would be my mate. Nico was meant to be with someone special to me. She meant the world to me. On that day, I challenged him more. I wanted him to be stronger to protect my sister Vixen. I needed him to be stronger for her because she wasn't an Alpha or a Beta. He was a perfect mate for Vixen. He would protect her. At the age of seventeen, Nico's wolf found his mate, and our family was so excited to have him in our family. Vixen always had a crush on him, so it was a quick mating for them. Nico is still one of my closest friends today.

Jared, however, was convinced that he was my mate. I knew he wasn't. I let him figure it out for himself. On in his seventeenth birthday, he came into the packhouse with a big smile, thinking it was going to be me as his mate. I was sitting at the table eating a chocolate PopTart. I looked up, and his smile faded, "Zoey, you aren't my mate." He was upset.

"Sorry, Jared!" I said, because I was. "You are still my closest friend and best pack enforcer. We will find them one day," as I got up and hugged him. That day changed our relationship; he became my brother. Jared later would be my sons' godfather.

I am thinking about other parts of my vision, so I didn't notice that someone walked into the cave and is currently standing looking at me in the cell. "I hear you thinking you are going to take him from me." I look up and standing in front of me with a smirk on her face is none other than Stefanie.

"It was you!" glaring at her. I hate this bitch

"Yes!" She is laughing.

"Why did you do this to me?" I need answers from this coward.

"Well, since you will never leave this cave alive, I might as well tell you the entire story...

"It all started three years ago. I went out with my girlfriends to the bar, and I ran into Colt. I knew as soon as I saw him, I wanted him. He came over and sat at our table. He talked to my friends and me for hours. He told us that he didn't find his mate yet. That he would know his mate when he saw her. After finding out he was the next Alpha of his pack, I made a decision then to put a plan into action to get him. I wanted to be Luna. All the power that comes with being Luna. We exchanged numbers that night. A couple days later, I called and asked him out on a date on the following Friday. He, of course, said yes! Why not! Look at me, I am fucking gorgeous."

I roll my eyes. "Just get on with it."

"That Friday we went out to dinner and had a couple drinks. When our drinks were done, he said, 'Thanks for a good night!' He was going to leave, so I used a potion that I had gotten from the witch. It knocked him out cold. With help, I got him back to my place. I undressed him and put him into my bed. He was so hot in my bed. I took out lotion and jerk him off and took his sperm. I froze it until he left the next day. When he woke up the next morning naked next to me, he thought we slept together. He apologized, 'This shouldn't of happen.' That he was 'waiting for his mate.' He got dressed in a hurry and left. That day I had an appointment at a clinic in Pittsburgh to have his sperm injected into me. Well, that was the plan. But it didn't go as planned. They informed me that I didn't have strong, viable eggs. The clinic could use another female wolf's eggs to complete the process. I couldn't give a child to my Alpha, but I could give birth to a child that would be his. They told me to talk to my Alpha mate, and if we agreed they would inseminate me in a couple days. I called the next day and agreed to the agreement. A couple days later, I went back to the clinic to be artificially inseminated. A week later, I found out I was indeed pregnant. So, I called Colt and told him I was pregnant with his child." All I could do is sit and listen to this crazy-ass story in disbelief. I knew she was the woman from the clinic. This fucking bitch is mine. She played us all. I just stared at her as she continued with her fucking confession.

"For the next couple of months, I lived with him, and he treated me well. I tried multiple times to sleep with him, but he gave me my own room. He wouldn't touch me; he was with me for the child. The day that fucking girl was born was the worst day of my life. He named her. She became his world. I was nothing to him, and I hated her for it. I begged him to claim me and make me his Luna. He always said, 'I am waiting for my fated mate.' So a week after the girl's birth, I went back to the witch and had her make a spell that would stop all mating rituals and conceiving pups. No one would have love until he claimed me as his mate and future Luna."

I had enough. I roared, "Her name is Meadow, not 'that girl.' And how did you get this witch to help you voluntarily? I don't understand why she would just help you. What would happen if his mate came along? I have so many questions, but I am completely sick by all the damage you have done to not only this pack but my family as well. I am going to kill you myself when I get out of here."

She was so proud of everything she was doing, so she continued, "Do you want to hear the rest? It feels good to tell someone. Everyone thinks I am a dumb blonde. I showed all of them. Getting back to my story… The witch didn't help me willingly. I kidnapped her sister, Dani. I have had her close to three years. She is my leverage. The witch you saw earlier she is my pawn. What is funny is she isn't really that old. She actually is a beautiful redhead around your age. Because she used dark magic, it is her curse." She just kept blabbing. I was disgusted by her. She just kept running her mouth. "When you and your friends came here, I saw how you were around him. So I watched you a lot. I tried to get him to stay away from you and that damn bar. It became his home, because even if he didn't know it, he wanted to be around you. He was dreaming about you. I heard him on multiple occasions. He talked about you to the girl. Then you befriended her and made her happy. I knew it was only a matter of time he would figure out that you are his mate because of the mate pull. Then the curse would be broken, and I wouldn't become Luna. I worked hard to get to this point. You see, his mate is the only person that can break the curse. If he willingly gives his heart to you and wants to mate with you, the curse is broken. Everything would return to normal, and I can't have that happen. So, the witch put a spell on your friend, and I drugged you to get you here. Now you know the entire store. By the way, I will never let you leave this cave. You will die here." Then she pointed at the bomb on the cave wall with a timer. She hit the button, and it started counting down. Fifteen minutes. "I will finally have everything I want. I will have the life you were supposed to have." As she smirked at me, "Goodbye, Zoey." She turned on her heels and walked out of the cave.

I scream, "I will get out of here and I am going to kill you, you fucking bitch."

As I am frantically looking around for a way out, I see a young redhead lying on a cot in a cell across from me. I'm yelling at her, but I get no response. She is probably drugged. I kneel and start to pray. "Moon Goddess, I have done everything you have ask of me up to this point. Please don't let me die like this. Help me, please!" In that split second, I see a bright light with an angelic voice coming from it.

"I am sorry, my child, for causing you so much pain. Zoey, I need to know, do you accept who you are from this moment? Do you promise to protect all wolves on earth and let my voice be heard? I need you to let your mate come to you. It must be his choice, free will, to be with you. If he accepts you as his Queen, the love and connection the two of you will share will be unmatched by any other wolf. You are no ordinary wolf; you have immense power within you. Colt is not only your soulmate but also your protector. Once you mate, both of you will become more powerful. You are not only his mate. You are his love, his heart, but most importantly his foundation. When one of you is out of control, the other will help the other stay grounded. The bond you will share in unbreakable. And if he chooses you, I will be back in one month to crown you as Queen of all wolves. You will reign with your equal mate beside you. We will have our first royal family in over three thousand years. A true love story for you both. I am trying to make up for my past mistakes. Do you agree to all of this, Zoey?"

Without thinking, "Yes!" I scream. When I again I feel a power filling me I never knew existed. The strength I have is overwhelming. I can't control the shift of my wolf. The cell doors open on their own. "Thank you, Moon Goddess!" Then I walk over to the cell where the young redhead is unconscious. I slide my head under her body and slide her down to the middle of my back. I take off running. I don't know how much time is left, but I know it can't be long before the bomb explodes. As I get to the entrance of the cave, the bomb explodes. It throws me, but I manage to keep the girl on my back. When I make it outside and slide her to the ground. The first thing I see is Tyson's wolf coming at me.

"Mom, are you okay?" He is mindlinking me while running. I see the worry in his eyes.

"I will be fine," and everything goes black.

COLT

I sit at the bar having a Miller Lite dreading going home. If it wasn't for Meadow, I would leave the pack for a while. Going home to listen to a woman bitch at me and I don't want anything to do with. I put my empty bottle out with more money. I need another so I can pass out when I get home. The bar doors open, and in comes in two young Alphas. They look familiar. They sit at the bar and order their drinks. Looking at them, I say, "Hey, I am Colt Reese. I haven't seen you two here before. You must be from the Westlyn pack."

The young one speaks first. "I am Tyson, and this is my older brother Derrick. We are Zoey Westlyn's sons."

"Nice to meet the two of you," I respond quickly, raising my bottle to them. As we make small talk, I realize I never ask Zoey about her mate. These two are definitely Alphas. I know the youngest one is the MMA champion, and my dad said that Derrick, the oldest, is a genius.

Derrick mentions, "Your Alpha is one of our pap's best friends. We loved coming here to visit when we were pups. They took us fishing, hunting, and gave us our first alcoholic drink. Alpha Craig is a good man." When he said that about my dad, it made me proud. I hope I can be as good an Alpha as he is. Every time I look at them, I see a lot of younger me in them. I laugh. Especially Derrick. Tyson looks a lot like Zoey. Derrick tells me about his company, his mate, and his pup on the way. Derrick's mate, Erica, is Alpha Knox's niece. She was raised by Knox and Luna Melody since birth because her parents, Creed and Callista, were killed by rouges three months after she was born. Creed was Knox's baby brother. The conversation comes so easy, like we have known each other for a while. I buy them both a drink. Tyson tells me about his title defense coming up in two months.

Finally, I had to ask the question that has been bothering me. "I know it's not my business, but what happen to your moms mate?"

As soon as I ask, they look at each other. Tyson looks at Derrick. "You want to tell him since that's why you are here."

Derrick speaks right away, "We don't know." I am stunned. I almost spit out my beer. But I don't say a word. I let him continue, "As kids, people made comments about her. Called her unkind names, but she took it. She never defended herself. 'Let them talk,' she would say. I have been asking her a lot lately, because my pup is coming. I need answers. So, I am here to get them from her. No more running away from the issue." He takes a big swig of his drink, but I can see the hurt in his eyes. The conversation is making Tyson uncomfortable, so he gets up to use the restroom. But when he returns, he is on the phone. His voice is getting loud and he is starting to use his Alpha voice. It captures Derrick and my attention. When he hangs up the phone, he says, "We have to go to the cabin now. Mom is missing, and no one can mindlink her. I tried to, and I am not getting a response. Derrick, it's not like Mom to do this."

Derrick agrees with him.

As they get up, I announce, "I am coming with you."

We get to the cabin fast and her friends are standing outside worried. Melina is crying, saying, "Something is wrong. She wouldn't just leave a note without mindlinking one of us. I just got back from our pack about an hour ago and tried to mindlink her. I didn't get a response." Holding a paper up to us, Melina continues, "This information is what she has been waiting for."

Sean says next, "Sasha and I tried to mindlink as well and nothing. She didn't come home last night. Her bed is still made."

Standing by the firepit, a man stalks out of the shadow of the woods. It's Zoey's friend Jared. I have seen him at pack meetings before. The boys call to him. "Uncle Jared," Derek yells. "When did you get here? Where is Mom? Have you seen her?"

He looks him in the eyes with no emotion. "She will be dead in about ten minutes. Did you know she found her mate and didn't tell anyone? She thought she should be punished for it." Everyone gasps. Melina's sobbing crying. Derrick takes off at him. Alpha speed, he is on him in seconds. The kids was beating the shit out of him. Jared took all the shots to the face and body. He didn't even try to defend himself.

Finally, I grab Derrick by the neck, pushing him off Jared. "Where is she at? Tell these boys where their mom is. If you care about these boys, tell them where she is." I am using my Alpha tone.

Jared looks at Tyson and says, "I am sorry! I couldn't do anything to stop her. She is in a cave on the southern part of the pack-lands."

Without a word both, the boys shift into their wolves, shredding their clothes. Their wolves were in control and pissed off. Wow! They were fucking enormous. They are large and true Alphas. They are bigger than me. One black and one white with the opposite color on the left front paw. When they took off, my wolf said, "Go! Protect!" Without a second thought, I shifted into my all-black wolf and ran to catch up to them. We arrived at the cave as the explodes. An all-white wolf is coming out with young woman on her back. Tyson is running to Zoey first.

Zoey drops the girl to the ground. She is looking at Tyson. He is growling at her. She says, "I will be fine." Then she drops to the ground unconscious, still in wolf form. She needs to go to the pack hospital. I shift back into my human form. I put the girl on Derrick's back and pick up Zoey. I look at the boys and say, "I know the fastest way to get them to the hospital." They nod their heads, and I take off running with two enormous wolves following me. As I am running, I mindlink my dad and have him send pack enforcers to collect Jared at the cabin. I want him taken to the dungeon below the packhouse. We will deal with him once Zoey is safe.

Arriving at the hospital, Dr. Aaron is waiting for us. He takes Zoey from me, and my wolf growls at him. Derrick and Tyson shift in their human form just look at me confused. The nurse brings the three of us scrubs to put on. It felt like forever, but I'm sure it was a half hour. The doctor enters the waiting room and informs us that they ran tests and don't understand why she isn't awake. She has a small levels of wolfsbane in her blood but nothing to keep her unconscious for a long period of time. Derrick is the first to voice his concern, "What do we do, Doctor? Can we see her?"

Doctor Aaron replies, "We wait and go ahead in to see her, but only two at a time." Dr. Aaron shows the boys to her room.

I keep myself busy, making phone calls to her friends, my family, my dad, and Zoey's parents. Alpha Zane said, "They were on their way. My dad called them when Zoey went missing."

I sit back in the chair in the waiting room and wait to hear from her sons. I want to be in her room to check on her. My wolf is getting antsy. Derrick walks out first. "If you want to go in and see her, go ahead," he says. He walks over to me and extends his hand to shake mine. "Thank you for helping our mom. She means the world to us. I will never forget what you have done for our family."

"Our family." When he said that, it shook something in me. My wolf calmed by this young man's acceptance of us.

As I enter her room, I see Tyson sitting beside her bed holding her hand. I can see the apprehension and uncertainty in his face as he is staring at his mom. Watching her lay unconscious, all I can think is she is one hell of a woman. She brings Alphas to their knees, including me. Tyson looks up at me and repeats the same thing his brother said earlier. As I stand at the bottom of her bed, all I can do is stare at her. I find myself praying she opens those beautiful green eyes. I want answers of what is happening.

The door flies open, revealing Zoey's parents. Her mother, Luna Violet, is at her bedside in seconds. Tears are rolling down her face; she pulls Zoey's falling hairs from her face and cries out loud. Alpha Zane is standing beside me with tears in his eyes, looking at his unconscious daughter. He turns to look at me, enraged, "Who would do this to my daughter? Zoey is everything

DARLENE MELLORS

good in this world. They will pay for this." I agree and tell him the entire story and about Jared. He calls to Zoey's mom. "Sweetheart, I am going to care of this. You look after our girl."

She responds, "Make them pay for this, Zane." A Luna is the heart of the pack, and she is pissed right now. I wouldn't want to piss off this Luna ever. Alpha Zane nods in agreement then turns to walk out the door, and I follow him.

We don't say a word to each other as we make our way to the dungeon. We see Jared sitting on the cot with hands on his head. Alpha Zane is growling. Jared looks up. "Alpha, I swear I didn't do this willingly. I think that witch cast a spell on me. I would never hurt Zoey. I love her." Now I growl at him. He looks at me. He says something that leaves me speechless. "The Moon Goddess chose a great mate for Zoey."

Alpha Zane opens the cell and walks over to Jared. "Did I hear you right? My Zoey found her mate?"

Jared says, "Yes! Please forgive me, Alpha. I would never hurt her or those boys."

Just as Alpha Zane was going to say something, his phone rings. He answers immediately, "Yes, Melina, let everyone know Colt and I will meet you in Alpha Craig's office in five minutes." He hangs up. "Colt, let's go. Jared we will be back later to talk to you." He turns to leave.

As I turn to follow, Jared says, "Colt, is she okay?" I don't answer. He continues, "Please protect her from that evil woman."

"Who?" I speak.

Then he says the name of the person who hurt my Zoey. "That bitch Stefanie. She did all of this." Looking at me, I know he is telling me the truth.

64

MELINA

Mom and I just left the hospital. She needs to get some sleep. Hell, we all do. Zoey wouldn't want us to fuss over her. Alpha Craig posted warriors outside her room, so she is safe. When I get to the cabin, I take a shower and put my pajamas on. I walk over to my bed and see an envelope sticking out from underneath my pillow. My name is on it in Zoey's handwriting. I open it to see instructions of what she wants done if something happens to her. I call my dad and inform him. He is going to meet me in Alpha Craig's office. I hang up and call the people on the list she left to be present for this. I collect all the paperwork, change my clothes, and head to the packhouse. Tonight many lives are going to change.

When I enter the office Alpha Craig, Alpha Knox, and Alpha Zander (my brother) are already present. I say hello to all of them. Soon after Erica, Derrick, Tyson, Sean, Sasha, Mom, Catie, Gage, and Meadow walk in at the same time. My dad and Colt are last to arrive. They both look pissed. Colt walks in and sits on one of the brown leather couches and pulls Meadow onto his lap. My dad walks over to the other Alphas, and they sit in the four chairs facing everyone else. The boys, Derrick and Tyson, stand behind the Alphas. The rest of the family take a seat on the remaining couches and chairs. As I am about to begin, in walks Cara and the asshole Chase. "Better late than never," I say, glaring at him. He makes a pretend hurt expression. Chase goes to stand behind Colt. I would love to fucking punch him in the face but this isn't about me. I need to do this for Zoey. I collect myself and start.

"Thank you, everyone, for coming on such short notice. Tonight when I got home from the hospital, I was getting ready to go to bed I found an envelope under my pillow addressed to me from Zoey." Everyone is shocked. My mom starts to cry. I know everyone is wondering what is going on. "In this"—I hold the envelope up—"Zoey ask for all of you to be present for the reading." I open the envelope; all eyes are on me. "If Melina is reading this, everything I know has come true. I have been injured, and there are secrets that need to be revealed to all of you in this room. I hope that you all will understand and accept what I have done to keep all of you safe the time has come for the truth to be told. After tonight, we will become one family of four packs." The four Alphas look at each other and smile.

"Only a few people know my secrets—all four Alphas, my mother, and my sister Melina. Please understand that I made them promise to keep my secrets. This is not their fault. I made this choice. My boys, I want to apologize for not telling you who your father is. Until recently, I didn't know myself. By the end of this letter, everything will be known to everyone in the room. It's time to hear the truth from me. It started when I was nineteen years old. I hadn't found my mate, and being an Alpha female, I can only be with my fated true mate. Also, I can only produce pups with my mate. So, one day I was at the fertility clinic, and Dr. Ames ask me about being artificially inseminated. He wanted to see if a new procedure would work on me with another Alpha. I refused right away but thanked him. My dream was always to have pups with my mate, not a stranger. That night, the Moon Goddess came to myself and everyone I mentioned above in a dream. She told us that I was to be artificially inseminated. It would make our packs stronger. Without hesitation, I was inseminated the next day. Four months later, Derrick was born. As you all know, Derrick is a true Alpha. He is the pup born by two Alphas. True Alpha's are rare; we haven't had one in over two thousand years. A true Alpha is born in four months after conception. Normal wolves are born in six months. Then three and a half years later, the Moon Goddess came to us again in a dream. I was inseminated the next day. Tyson was born four months later. Again, a true Alpha. Dr. Ames told me that I am the only one that the procedure worked for. Boys, the reason I never got upset is because the Moon Goddess had a plan for us, and I never questioned it. Years later, being a doctor, Melina and I figured out why I was the only one to produce true Alphas. The Alpha that donated his sperm is my fated true mate. I know all of this is surprising. Imagine my surprise that my other half is my boys' father. He donated his sperm anonymously. I have been trying to find him for the last eighteen years. Boys, I love you both with all my heart, but knowing I had a part of my mate in both of you, this made my wolf and I feel truly grateful. I thank the Moon Goddess every day for both of you. When I came to the Reese pack, I did in fact find my mated true mate. Please don't be upset, but I had your Aunt Melina collect DNA from all of you. She stole your toothbrushes. Ha ha! The night I disappeared, she went back to our pack to run a DNA test to see if what I knew was true. As for my mate, he doesn't recognize me as his mate due to this pack fertility-mating issue. Melina, hand my sons the DNA results, please. Before you open them, I want you to know that your father is a kind, loving, and good man. You both are a lot like him."

Derrick and Tyson both look at the envelopes I just gave them. Tyson smiles and looks to Derrick. "It makes sense now." Derrick nods with an even bigger grin on his face. I know that Derrick has been pushing Zoey lately for answers. He will finally have them.

My dad is the first to speak, "Well, who is your father?" They look at each other and smirk. At the same time, the boys shout, "Colt!" Everyone is shocked and speechless except Colt and Alpha Craig.

Colt is the first to speak. "I did donate sperm over twenty-four years ago. The Moon Goddess came to me in my sleep and told me to do it for the betterment of the packs. I have kept this secret all this time."

No one said a word, they just stared at him.

"Okay, everyone, there is a lot more to this. Can I get the next part of what Zoey has here?" Pointing at the papers.

"Boys, I hope you can understand all of this. I never meant to keep this from you. What you are about to hear is even more surprising. Three years ago, the Moon Goddess came to me again. It was my turn to return the favor. I was to donate my eggs to a female wolf that couldn't conceive with her Alpha husband. A couple days later, that female walked into the clinic. Melina came to me, and without hesitation, I donated my eggs. Once she was inseminated, we never heard from her again. Well, I take that back. Recently, she called to ask for me to donate again and it bothered me. She had one child; shouldn't she feel blessed to have that child? A couple days later, we came to the Reese pack. So I never got to respond to her. The first day I was here, I met this beautiful little girl who has my eyes. I felt a connection to her like my sons. I couldn't explain it at first. Then her daddy pulled in and got out of the truck, and my wolf yelled, 'MINE!' My mate didn't recognize me. It hurt. I have never felt such happiness and hurt in my life. It took a little while, but I figured out that the pack issues were magical, not medical. My wolf and I yearned to spend more time with Meadow. I needed to protect her. I asked Melina to do a DNA on Meadow as well. I wanted to know if what I was feeling was true. Today, Meadow and I went for a walk to get away from the packhouse because she heard Stefanie and Colt fighting. She asked me to show her my wolf. Of course, I did. I couldn't say no to her. What happened next, I was sure she was my daughter. She let her wolf out for me. We all know a pup's first shift is with her Alpha or her mother. She gave me the honor to be the first to see her wolf. She is so much like brothers. They did the same thing with me. In case you're all wondering, she is a beautiful white wolf with two black front paws . I know you all are overwhelmed by all this information, but Meadow already knows, and I asked her to keep it a secret until we had the DNA results. I am one hundred percent positive that Stefanie is the woman from the clinic. She is hungry for the power being Luna. She planned everything down to even getting rid of me. Melina, could you please give Colt the DNA test?"

Colt opens the envelope and laughs, "It's true! She is Zoey's daughter."

Meadow says to Colt, "Daddy, Mommy says I am beautiful and a princess." Colt hugs her, and I swear I see tears in his eyes.

"Can I continue, please? There is more." Everyone nods. "As I sit here writing this, I find myself giggling. I am a forty-four-year-old virgin with three children to my fated true mate. My sons have had sex before me. I saved myself for my other half. No one else would have what belongs to him. He will have me mind, body, and soul. I have waited my entire life for him. From the first moment I saw him, tall, dark and handsome, I would love him forever. I believe in the Moon Goddess's plan for all of us.

What I am going to ask next will be a lot, but please take it easy on Jared, Jarrah, and Dani. They were pawns in Stefanie's plan. She is a power-hungry bitch. She used this pack and my family to her benefit. She hurt my daughter every day. I will make her pay for everything she has done to us. You all have my word on this. Jared had a spell cast on him and Jarrah did what she had to do to protect her sister. Dani was kept prisoner for over two and a half years. I forgive them, and all of you should try as well. They are our family."

Just as I'm getting ready to read more from Zoey, the door to the office opens. It's Stefanie! "I have been looking for my daughter," she said, but you could tell she was nervous. As she starts to walk over to Meadow, I hear a loud growl from the other side of the room. It's Zoey walking in from the back door. Wow! She looks great! Like nothing ever happened to her.

"If you touch my daughter, I will kill you on that spot," She is one pissed-off mama wolf. Making her way over to stand right in front of Stefanie.

"Your daughter, right." Stefanie laughs. Zoey doesn't look away from Stefanie but says, "Colt, show her." He hands the DNA results to her. Colt's eyes are black; that is a pissed-off daddy. Alpha Craig calls for Diesel, the Pack Beta, to take Stefanie to the dungeon.

Stefanie steps to Zoey, looking her right in the eyes and says, "You haven't heard the last of me. You ruined everything for me. I will kill you and your daughter."

Zoey growls. "Try anything with my daughter and I will kill you, bitch!" Then Zoey punches her in the face and Stefanie goes flying across the room into the wall. The wall shatters like glass. That is the power of an Alpha and pissed off mama. Diesel picks up and unconscious Stefanie and takes her away.

ZOEY

Knocking Stefanie's ass out felt so good. After waking up in the cold, sterile room, I knew I was in the hospital. Taking all the wires off me, a man came running into the room. You could see the worry in his face subside when he saw me sitting up on the bed. I woke up to a bad vision. I had to get to the office to protect my daughter. The doctor gave me an all clear that I could go. I used my Alpha tone, "Get my clothes, now!" A nurse brought me in a set of scrubs, and I was out the door within minutes. This bitch has hurt my family, but more importantly my daughter. Meadow got up and ran to me. I lean down and calmly say, "She will never hurt you again, baby."

She is looking down at the ground and mumbles, "Yes, mama!"

I put my fingers under her chin and lift her face to look me in the eyes. "Meadow, from this day, you will never look down when you speak or are spoken to. You are the daughter, sister, niece, and granddaughter of the greatest Alphas. My princess, you are the best of your daddy and I," I calmly say, trying to be strong but not angry. Stefanie screwed my daughter up.

"Okay, Mama!" She beams at me. I kiss her head. "Good, princess! Now go over and sit next to your daddy." I have something I need to do and say. She walks over to the couch and sits down. I stand up and look directly at my boys. They are standing behind my daddy. They walk over to me. I need a hug from them. I've missed them.

Tyson is the first to open his mouth, "You really okay, Mom?" I nod.

Derrick is next. "I love you and could never be mad at you for this."

"Thank you. I love you both." As I am hugging them both tightly. Tyson doesn't want to let me go. Squeezing me, I whisper, "I can't breathe Tyson."

"Sorry, Mom! I just missed you so much. I don't know what I would do without you." I am thrown by his expression of tenderness. "Don't worry, I am not going anywhere." I wink at him.

My mom is next. She stands up and hugs me. "I would have killed her," she mindlinks me.

"I know, Mom!" I reply, backing away, knowing she truly would have. I turn around to see the Alphas all standing. They bow to me. I hope no one noticed. I walk to all of them and hug Knox, Zander, Craig, and Daddy.

Dad hugs me tighter and whispers, "I love you, my Queen." I pull away from the hug and kiss him on the cheek.

"Still your little girl, Daddy," I whisper back and wink.

He laughs, "Yes, you are!"

I look over my friends, blow them a kiss. "We are drinking some alcohol later."

"Hell yeah," Sean and Sasha say in unison.

I look over at Melina. I can tell she has been crying. "I have someone who has been waiting," as I look her in the eyes feeling her emotions. I walk out of the room. In an instant I return carrying the most adorable dark-midnight-haired, blue-eyed four-year-old boy. "He missed his mama!" She looks at me as if she is in shock. "No peeking Chance!" I whisper and he comes back with.

"I promise, Aunt Zoey!" I make my way to stand to front of Melina. "Open your eyes, Chance."

"Mommy!" he screams with so much excitement. Melina takes her baby boy in her arms. I had Vixen, Nico, my nephew Dakota, and my niece Zuri bring Chance here. I wanted our family all together tonight. After a couple seconds, Chance looks at me, "Zoey, I heard Mommy say that you found your mate?" He sounds upset.

"I did, baby! What is wrong?" Watching him carefully.

"Am I still your special guy?"

Everyone busts out laughing. I take him from Melina. "Chance, you are one of two special boys to me. Do you want to know why?" He shrugs. "You and Dakota are not only my nephews, but you are also both my godsons. You have a special place right here." As I point to my chest, he hugs me tight, and I know he is satisfied with my answer. I return him back to his mom.

COLT

As we are all sitting listening to Melina tell us what Zoey has written for all of us to hear, I remember the Moon Goddess coming to me in a dream, asking me to donate my sperm; with no questions, I did as she wanted and never second guessed her. When Melina said that Zoey was inseminated with Alpha sperm. I found myself hoping that it was mine. As soon as the boys read the results to the DNA tests, I couldn't be happier. These young men are my sons. I looked at them with tears of joy in my eyes. Derrick is all me, and Tyson is definitely his mom. They are our true Alphas. If that wasn't enough, I am hit with the realization that I am going to be a grandfather. Erica, Derrick's mate, is due in two months. I look over at her and she is staring at me with a genuine smile. Then she winks at me. This beautiful young woman has long, flowing brown hair with the bluest eyes. The Moon Goddess has blessed my son with a kind and compassionate woman as his mate. She will be an incredible Luna someday. Looking back to my pups, I can't help but be proud of Zoey for raising such remarkable young men. From today, I am going to make a point to spend a lot of time with them. I want to know everything about my sons. "My sons," as I smile from ear to ear.

When Melina said that I am Zoey's fated true mate, I was thrown a bit. Fated true mates are rare. As far as I can remember, there hasn't been true mates in almost a century. Then she brought up how Zoey was told by the Moon Goddess to donate her eggs to an Alpha and his mate because they couldn't conceive. Why would she ask her such a thing? She is my mate and should only have our pups. Then I am hit with another realization of how much I hurt my mate. She felt the bond from the beginning. What pain did I put her through? I never want to cause her any pain. I am pissed at myself for doing this to her. I didn't feel the mate bond. My wolf always gets aroused when she is around. But in my dreams, I am drawn to her. Maybe my wolf was trying to tell me subconsciously. It must be this damn curse on our pack. I am interrupted from my thoughts when Melina informs us that Meadow shifted for Zoey. I am confused. She would only shift for the first time, with her Alpha, my dad, or her mother. Zoey is Meadow's mother? It can't be true. Melina hands me the DNA results. I hurriedly open them, and it's all in black and white. 99.9 percent Zoey is Meadow's mother. My mate is the mother of all three of my pups. I have three pups. I am in utter disbelief.

Meadow says, "Mom says I am beautiful and a princess." I have never seen her so happy. I am overcome again with emotion. When Melina starts talking again, I am thrown for another loop. My mate saved herself for me. She is still a virgin. I guess I am too. Since I never slept with Stefanie. Knowing this makes my wolf ecstatic, continuing to listen to what Zoey says, I also understand and will try to forgive Jared and Jarrah. It will take time, but if Zoey can do it, I will try as well. Jarrah was protecting her sister. I would do anything to protect the ones I love.

We are all shocked to see the office door swing open and Stefanie running in. This bitch has some big balls coming in here for my daughter; she hurt my baby for the last time. Before I can do or say anything, we all hear a loud growl coming from the back door of the office. There she is…my Zoey! Her eyes are glowing bright green. Even in the hospital scrubs she looks beautiful but pissed. Zoey walks straight up to Stefanie. Standing inches apart, Zoey looks her in the eyes. "If you touch my daughter, I will kill you on that spot."

Stefanie laughs, "Your daughter, right!"

Zoey doesn't take her eyes off Stefanie but says, "Colt, show her!" I hand Stefanie the DNA results; my wolf wants to take over and kill the bitch. My dad calls for Diesel to take Stefanie to the dungeon. Before Diesel gets to her, Stefanie says something to Zoey and Zoey punches her right in the face. Stefanie goes flying across the room like a rag doll and shatters the plastered wall.

Wow! This woman is definitely a powerful Alpha female. She may have more strength than me. Zoey looks calmer when Diesel picks up the unconscious bitch and takes her away. Meadow runs over to her mom. She is so excited to see her. The connection they have, why didn't I notice it before now? We all watch in awe at the bond shared between them. Zoey lifts Meadow's face with her finger to look Zoey in the eyes.

Calmly, she says, "Meadow, from this day you will never look down when you speak or are spoken too. You are the daughter, sister, niece, and granddaughter to the greatest Alphas. You, my daughter, are the best of your daddy and me." Meadow comes over to sit beside me. I kiss her head, but I notice that Zoey isn't looking at me. She is avoiding me. Did I hurt her that bad? Does she hate me or regret me as her mate? The boys walk over to her. I can see how much they mean to her. Both of them are hugging her. I swear Tyson isn't going to let her go. Derrick and Tyson hear "I love you both," and they relax. Zoey and her mom must of mindlinked each other. They are looking at each other with hazy, glossy eyes. When Zoey turns to the four Alphas, all four bow to her. Why would they do that? Alphas don't bow to anyone. Wait! There is only one person an Alpha bows to. It can't be. Oh fuck! She can't be! My mate is the Queen Alpha! I think back to when I was younger. My dad told us the legend of the Queen Alpha. "The Queen Alpha is a white wolf. She will have immense power. She will do incredible things for our kind. The Queen Alpha will have only one fated true mate, and he will also be her protector. He will be the only wolf that will be stronger than her. Her mate, after their mating ceremony and marking each other, will have special abilities of his own. He will be a master in combat and weapons. He will protect his Queen with his life." It's me! I am the Queen's protector. I am lost in my own mind when I see Zoey walk out the door. When she returns with a little blue-eyed, coal dark-haired little boy. I hear a low growl coming from directly behind me. It's Chase. Who does this boy belong to? Why is Chase pissed? What the fuck is going on? What did I miss? Looking around the room for answers. Then the young pup calls Melina

"Mommy." Oh shit, she has a four-year-old. You can see how much he loves Melina and Zoey. His name is Chance.

He asks Zoey, "Aunt Zoey. I heard Mommy say you found your mate? Am I still your special guy?" Everyone laughs. I like this pup. He has no filter. You can see how much they care for each other. Zoey explains everything to him. He accepts what she says, and Zoey hands him back to Melina. I catch Melina look over my direction. She is looking right at Chase, and I look over my shoulder to see a pissed-off, growling Chase. It was a low growl, but I could hear it. What is up with these two?

Breaking the tension in the room, Derrick walks over and stands beside his mom. Zoey puts her arm around his waist and smiles. He looks around the rooms and speaks. "Standing here, it hit me. I am related to all of the Alphas. Alpha Zane and Alpha Craig are my grandfathers, Alpha Zander is my uncle. And Alpha Knox is Erica's uncle, but more like her father since he has raised her since she was three months old."

Zoey looks at him and smiles. "One family, four packs." She points at Knox, Zane and my dad. "These three Alphas have been friends since they were pups. What you all might not know is the Alphas' mates come from the Easton pack, my grandfather's pack. Violet, Melody, and Daisy were best friends. They met their Alpha mates at the Tempest when they were seventeen; they all mated, and the rest is history."

The Alphas all agreed.

"What is the Tempest?" Derrick asks.

"Well, up until Daisy died, it was where all four packs met on the full moon every month to see if your mate was from one of the other packs. It was a celebration for the young pups turning seventeen. Coming into their wolves and for the ones that found their mates, it was a mating ritual. They stood before the Moon Goddess to declare their love and lifetime bond to each other." Zoey smiled at the Alphas and asks "Is that right, Alphas?"

They all nodded in agreement.

"I didn't know anything about that why did we stop after Daisy, I mean, my grandmother died." He looked at me not knowing how I would react. I nodded to him that it was okay. She would be so happy to be a grandmother. I miss her. I know the triplets miss her more because I at least had her in my life for four years.

Then I heard my dad's voice. "It was my doing. When I lost Daisy, I didn't want to go there anymore and see everyone else happy with their mates. I was bitter for a long time. With that being said, I would love to start that tradition again. I feel a lot of people may have missed their mates because of my foolishness."

Zoey jumped in right away. "Don't ever be sorry for missing your mate; she was your other half. Even though she wasn't your fated mate, once you marked each other you became one. It still hurt. Daisy would be proud of you and the pups you raised. My godmother loved everyone and never had a harsh word to say about anything or anyone. She loved us all.

Dad walked over to Zoey who had tears in her eyes and hugged her tight. "You are an incredible woman, Zoey. We are all blessed to have you as our…" She looked up at him, shaking her head no.

ZOEY

Craig almost gave my secret away because he was a little too emotional. I backed away but couldn't look at Colt. What would I see? Would he be mad at me for knowing he was my mate, about the boys, or how he felt about me being Meadow's mom? My dad got up out of his chair and walked over to me and whispered, "Zoey, it's time, sweetheart. Everyone in this room loves you, and your last secret is safe to tell them. I don't know how much longer we can keep it from them." I mindlink and tell him to do it because I am afraid of what they will think of me. "I want to apologize for not telling a lot of people that Zoey is an Alpha female. The other Alphas and I decided together to keep it to ourselves and our most trusted friends. We had our reasons. She is our daughter, so Violet and I did what was best to protect her. The first time we knew Zoey was different she was about three years old. She got into a fight with another pup and I used my Alpha tone on her, but it didn't work. As she grew older, none of the Alphas have been able to control her with our orders. Trust us, we tried. Then as a teenager, her commands were irresistible to anyone, including us Alphas. We all knew how special our Zoey really was. Zoey is so much more than an Alpha female." Everyone listened closely as my daddy spoke. "She's the Queen Alpha!" I looked over in shock to see who said it. It was Colt!

Looking him straight in the eyes. "How did you know? Have you known?" I couldn't get a vibe on him. Was he upset or happy? He isn't showing any emotion.

"I figured it out," he replied calmly. My sons, on the other hand, are looking at me in jaw-dropping awe. Sean and Sasha looking much the same.

"Remember the stories and legends of the Queen Alpha I told

you two as pups." I look to my boys. "Well, it's true. I am the Queen Alpha. The one chosen by the Moon Goddess." I start to look around the room at everyone.

Derrick interrupts, "How long have you known? Do you really have special powers from the Moon Goddess? The stories you told us about were brains, brawn, beauty, and beasts. What does that mean? What does all this mean, Mom? Do I still call you mom or my Queen?" He is so overwhelmed right now. He keeps dropping more questions before I can answer.

Tyson jumps in, "Derrick, let her answer one question before you keep asking another." He looks to me and says, "Go ahead, Mom!" I take a deep breath.

"First of all, I did all of this to protect you both. I have known my entire life who I am. That is why I trained harder and trained both of you to persevere as well. Tyson is the only fighter in human and wolf form that has come close to beating me." Tyson beams at me with pride on the compliment. "Secondly, I do have special powers. I can heal quickly, telepathic, premonition, can use white magic, lie detection, strength, speed, agility, and being the fiercest of all wolves."

Derrick laughs and says, "I knew you had powers. You always knew when I lied. It was weird how you always knew!"

"I don't have all my powers yet. I won't have them all until my fated true mate and I mark each other. Then at my coronation is when all my powers will be completely bestowed upon me. And for all of you here, the headaches I get, they are premonitions. They aren't headaches at all. They hurt sometimes, well, not anymore. A little girl's touch makes them easier to have." Everyone looks at Meadow disbelief. I smile at my little girl, who is starting to look tired. "As for the brains, that would be you." I point at Derek. "The brawn would be Tyson, the beauty is Meadow. As for the beasts, they aren't here yet." I blush, and everyone in the room stares at me. I know they are comprehending everything I just said. "As for you, calling me anything other than Mom will piss me off. I growl a little. Do you three understand me?" All three of my pups nod in agreement. With perfect timing,

Meadow stands up and walks over to her brothers. Derrick and Tyson kneel down and hug their baby sister for the first time. Looking away from them, I see everyone including Colt with tears of joy in their eyes. When the boys stand up, Tyson picks up Meadow, hugging her tight! "I need to say somethings that are important for all of you to hear." All eyes are on me. "Dad, as of today the next Alpha of the Westlyn pack will be Derrick. I am passing my title to the pack to him."

My dad walks over to Derrick, slaps him on the back, and announces, "Our pack couldn't be in better hands."

"Alpha Knox, Tyson will be going back to the King pack to help you with your rouge problems." "It will be an honor to have your help son." Knox hugs Tyson, looks at me, and winks. Knox knows that the rouge issue isn't the only reason I am sending Tyson with him.

"My coronation will be at the next full moon. That is exactly one month from today at the Tempest. I have already started preparations for my coronation. I am also resuming the mating ritual ceremony again at the Tempest as a monthly event for all four packs. Anyone have anything to say?" Surprisingly, everyone is in agreement. I knew it has to be done; I am just glad everyone is on board. One month from today, I will become the first Queen Alpha in over three thousand years.

"If you all don't mind, I would like to put my daughter to bed. She looks exhausted. I am also in need of a drink, so I will meet whoever wants to have a couple drinks at the cabin in about an hour." As I take Meadow from Tyson and walk out of the office, Melina is right behind me with Chance on her hip. I need to talk to her about Chase. Also, tonight, we have to sit and discuss her becoming my Right Hand. If she accepts the title, she will be my most trusted confidant. Like she isn't already. This will make it official. Being blessed by the Moon Goddess and marked with a tattoo binding us for life, I wouldn't want it to be anyone else.

As we walk into Meadow's room, I change my mind about leaving her here. I want her close to me. I find a small suitcase and pack a few things, and the four of us walk down the back staircase heading towards the cabin. As we are making our way to the cabin, Melina is the first to break the silence. "Zoey, what is going on in the mind of yours?" I turn my head to look at her but continue to walk toward our destination.

"Melina, I know about you and Chase remember. I have my visions, so I have seen everything. You don't need to explain anything to me. When you want to talk about it, I will be here to listen. I won't push you." She doesn't say a word, just nods her head, excepting what I have just expressed to her. We make it to the cabin when I suggest, "Let's get the pups bathed and in bed, then you and I will talk more about my coronation."

Melina grins and says, "Okay!" I knew she wanted to discuss this further. She has always been inquisitive even since we were pups almost nosy!

Once the pups are bathed and in their pajamas, I take Meadow to my room and lay her in my king-size bed. Ever since I found out she is my daughter; I want to keep her close to protect her. As I cover her up, I look at my beautiful, long dark-haired, green-eyed little girl who is really my daughter. I whisper, "Thank you, Moon Goddess, for such a blessing."

Meadow shyly looks at me. "Can I have a kiss goodnight, Mommy?" I love hearing her call me Mommy.

"Of course, sweetheart," I reply with tears in my eyes. I lean down and kiss her cheek and hug her so tight. "I love you, princess. Now get some sleep. I will be outside if you need me."

As I am about to turn away, I feel and smell him. "Can I get a kiss too?" Colt speaks in such a loving and caring tone while making his way over to the bed from the doorway. I wonder how long he has been standing there. I step back for him to kiss our daughter. Meadow smiles at us both. "Goodnight, Mommy and Daddy! I love you both!" My heart is so full and thankful looking at our precious little girl. Colt and I turn walk out the bedroom door. I close it. Colt is standing in my way like a roadblock.

"I didn't expect you to be here," trying to hide my emotions around him. The more Colt is around, the harder it is getting for me. But I have to keep reminding myself that it has to be his choice.

"I want to be around my mate and spend time with my pups. I can't believe how much our lives have changed today." He is finally starting to open up to me. Wait! Did he just call me his mate? He smiles and continues, "Come on, let's go outside sit by the fire and talk." He extends his hand out for me to take. When I take it, an electric shock consumes my entire body. He has only touched me once before, but this time it feels different. It's an amazing sensation. I know he feels it as well. When I look at his eyes, they have gone black. Colt blurts out, "Wow, that feels... well, I have never felt anything so amazing in my life. Zoey, let's go outside before we do something we will both regret. I mean, our daughter is on the other side of that door and our sons are right outside. I can smell your arousal, and it's driving my wolf and I crazy." We agree and walk hand-in-hand outside. This right here is what I always wanted, and I never want it to end.

When we walk outside and over to the firepit, we see our boys, Erica, Melina, Sean, and Sasha sitting around it already. Derrick mentions about what a beautiful place this is. Colt replies, "Thank you! I built this cabin twenty years ago for my mate and pups. So, I guess it's your home."

I stood there with my mouth hanging open in disbelief.

"There is a first! Mom is shocked and speechless. I don't think that has ever happen!" Tyson announces while busting a gut. Everyone else joins in at my expense.

"Zoey, you're my mate, and our pups are here now. You can always stay here or at the pack house, it's your choice."

As soon as Colt says it, I come right back with, "I would love to stay here. It's absolutely gorgeous here. I thought that the first day I walked in here."

"I remember what you said to my dad." Colt grinned at me and winked. Oh my, I am a goner, he is so hot!

"And ours," my horny wolf claims.

COLT

Standing outside the bedroom door, I intently watch my two girls. Meadow is so happy being with her real mom. I can see the bond they have already. After we say goodnight to our daughter, we step out of the room. Zoey turns to close the door. For the first time, my wolf claims Zoey as "Mine!" As soon as he says it, I feel different. My wolf and I feel so much love for her. I feel the bond to her. When Zoey took my hand, I felt the sparks. An electric current went through my entire body. My wolf said, "Mate!" He wants to claim her right now. I had to push him back. I blurted out with even thinking. "Wow, that feels…well, I have never felt anything so amazing in my life. Zoey, let's go outside before we do something we will both regret. I mean, our daughter is on the other side of that door and our sons are right outside. I can smell your arousal, and it's driving my wolf and I crazy." Her pineapple-and-mango scent is now my favorite fragrance. As we walk hand-in-hand outside, all I can do is thank the Moon Goddess for blessing me with an incredible mate. I hope she wants to stay here with me. The woman already has my heart. The feelings are new and amazing. I never imagined that it would be this perfect. Finding my mate and having pups brings my wolf calmness. Although he is acting like a horny schoolboy, he keeps telling me to claim her now, so everyone knows that she is ours.

When Derrick brings up the cabin, I am overjoyed that he thinks it's beautiful. "Thank you!" comes out of my mouth before I can think. I built this house for them. Everyone laughs when Tyson says, "There is a first, Mom is shocked and speechless. I don't think that has ever happened." I am watching her closely. She is truly shocked.

Looking at her, "Zoey, you are my mate, and our pups are here now. You can always stay here or at the packhouse. It's your choice."

"I would love to stay here. It's absolutely gorgeous here. I thought that the first day I walked in here," she excitedly replied.

"I remember what you said to my dad," smiling at her with a wink. I could immediately smell her arousal again. Good to know what I can do to my mate, because she does the same thing to me. Zoey leaves me to walk over to the bar to get a beer. I make my way to the loveseat beside my sons. Zoey makes her way over and hands me a vodka and cranberry. She sits down with me. I look around and am suddenly overcome again with joy. This is what I always dreamed of. I feel complete. As we sit together, I get to hear everything about my sons. From the time they were born, as pups, as teenagers, and how they are doing now. My oldest son told me how he met Erica through a friend on St. Paddy's Day. "The moment my eyes met hers, my wolf screamed 'mate!'"

And Tyson told me how he got into MMA fighting. "Well, Mom beat me for the fifteenth time, and I couldn't stand losing to a girl. Let alone my mom. So I went out, convinced I would never lose to another person. She drove me to be better. I guess we all know why." I look up to see a man walking out of the woods toward us Jared! Why is he here now? My wolf doesn't feel any hostility coming from him, so I put my arm around my mate to show him she is mine. He looks me in the eyes and, surprisingly, bows his head to me. He is giving me respect because I am an Alpha. Maybe he isn't really a bad guy. Zoey wants us to forgive him. I am going to try for her. I give him a smile, and he continues to walk over. He sits in the chair across from Zoey and me.

Jared looks at Zoey and pleads, "I am so sorry for what I did to all of you. Zoey, I will understand if can't forgive me. Just know that I love you all. You're my family. I wouldn't willingly do anything to hurt any of you. And, Colt, I meant what I said in the dungeon. The Moon Goddess chose a great mate for Zoey."

I can see it in his eyes and hear it in his voice that he means every word. Zoey smiles at him and replies, "I know. I already forgave you. Jared, you couldn't control the spell. Even though none of these guys thought about it, you saved me. Thank you for telling my guys where I was at. If you wouldn't have told them where I was, they may not have made it in time. You are like a brother to me and godfather to my sons. I know it was the spell, not you." Zoey turns to look at me. "You know I am right." Then she looks at everyone else. "It's over! We move on from here. The guilty party is in the dungeon. Dani is alive and finally awake. I want you all to let it go for me." Everyone agrees with her. This woman is amazing. I lean in to kiss her cheek. As I do, she turns her face to me, and our lips touch. Wow! She brings her hands to my face and deepens the kiss. I am consumed by her touch and scent. She opens her mouth, and I slip my tongue in. I am in heaven. Sparks and electric flow through my entire body. I hear her moan. When I lean back to look at her, I see the most intense, bright green eyes looking at me with so much love. Her wolf is coming to the surface. I know exactly how she feels. I reach out and touch her face.

"You're beautiful, baby!" whispering to her.

She blushes. "That was a perfect first kiss." She is still blushing, looking at me with want and need. My wolf and I feel the pull getting stronger. "Get a room! I don't want to see my parents making out. I will be scarred for life," Tyson yells with a big smile on his face. It interrupts our moment we are having. Everyone chuckles as Erica, Sasha, and Melina congratulate Zoey on finally finding her mate. The guys say the same to me.

The women are hugging Zoey when Erica turns to Derrick and says, "Honey, I am exhausted. Can we go to bed please?" Derrick gets up grabs his mate's hand and walks into the cabin. He is going to be a good Alpha and an incredible father. I am so proud to be his dad. Soon, everyone else stands to leave saying their goodnights. I know Zoey wants to talk to Melina, but I don't want to leave her. I stand, kiss her on her forehead, and walk into the cabin to check on Meadow. As I enter the bedroom, our bedroom, the one I built for us. All I want to do is sleep. I move Meadow to the middle and lay down beside her. Calmness and peace is all I feel. Before I know it, I am out like a light.

ZOEY

When Colt goes into the cabin, I make my way over to the bar. Pulling out two shot, glasses Melina walks over and sits across the bar from me. I hand her a shot of blue raspberry and Red Bull. I pour myself a shot of Kinky. We raise out shots and toast, "Here is to finding our happily ever after!"

Melina laughs. "Maybe you, not me!" We both down the shots. Now I need to talk to my ride-or-die, sister, and beffer about another change coming in her crazy life.

Melina beats me to the punch. "Zoey, I know you have things you want to talk to me about, but I need to tell you about the stuff I found out as well. Please let me go first?" I know she is serious and piqued my curiosity. She continues, "When I went back to our pack to do the DNA tests on your pups, I was waiting for the test results when I started reading. I came across a little brown book peeking out from behind some of my fertility books. I have no idea where it came from. I opened it up to see two words: Queen Alpha. In the book, it described everything about your powers, your weakness, your mate, mating ceremony, and right hand. I also learned and was surprised to see that many kinds of blessed wolves in our world. They come from a royal bloodline of pure bloods. Our family are royal pure bloods! The family of purebloods are Westlyns! You were chosen by the Moon Goddess to be our Queen Alpha. The first Queen came into existence about four thousand years ago. The only Queen to be accepted by her mate. The Queen and her mate are the most beloved and powerful of our kind. Although feared by all other species. All your powers will be given to you when you and your fated true mate consummate your union sexually and by marking each other. The

Moon Goddess will bestow your powers to you and your mate at the mating ritual. Your mate will come into his powers, but it didn't have exactly what they may be. He will also be your protector. Your protector will guard you and your family with his life." As I sit here listening to Melina, I know she has more information to tell me.

"Unlike normal mating ceremonies, you and your mate have to mate within a time window of forty-eight hours or the bond between you will sever. Neither will have a second-chance mate. With normal mating wolves, we don't have time frames, and most get a second-chance mate. I am sorry, Zoey! As long as you and Colt mate, truly become one, the two of you are of one mind, body, and soul, your bloodline will be the strongest of our kind. Your heirs are powerful as well. Each of them will fully come into their own powers when you receive yours. Just like you, they will be immune to silver and wolfsbane. As for your 'Right Hand' I didn't see much on that."

I stop her from going any further. Now it's my turn to tell her what I know. "Mel, I know what you want to know about my 'Right Hand'! The person who will become my right hand will be a person I trust completely with all my secrets and will protect everyone I love. This position is a great honor to be bestowed upon them. This person will give it to me straight and have no lies between us. At my coronation, the Moon Goddess will bless us. We will say sacred vows, and be tattooed, which will bind us together for life." I watch her closely, knowing her mind is comprehending everything I just said. She looks at me and smiles.

"Colt is the perfect person for that. He is your mate, after all." I know she genuinely means it. "No, Colt will not be my 'Right Hand.' He is my mate, father of my pups, and my protector. Colt will always try to protect me because of love. I need someone who will be completely honest with me, good or bad. I want someone who I have trusted my entire life. The person who loves my pups as much as I do. She tells me like it is even when I don't want to hear it. She is the only person I want standing beside me. So, with that being said, Mel, will you do me the honor of being my right hand?"

"Well, I never saw that coming. I need another shot!" She is shocked. I pour us another shot. Mel looks at me in disbelief. "You really want me to do this for you?"

"Yes, you are the first and only person I want beside me. You were brought into my life for a reason. I believe this is it. We are family. We share the same bloodline. I trust you above anyone else."

Mel lifts her glass, looks at me with tears in her eyes. "It would be my honor, my Queen. Whatever you want or need I will have your back." We down our shots, and I walk around the bar and hug her tightly.

"I love you, beffer! We are going to do incredible things together," I respond with tears in my eyes. The Moon Goddess gave me an unbelievable person to stand beside me.

We sit by the firepit for a couple hours crying and laughing about the situations we have been through over the last week. I don't bring up Chase at all. "Zoey, I see how Colt looks at you. I believe he feels the mate bond. The way he was looking at you tonight in the office was every woman's dream. Melt your panties look."

I roll my eyes at her.

"When are you two going to have your mating ceremony?"

"I don't know, Melina. Colt and I need to talk about it tomorrow. The Moon Goddess says it must be free will and it's his choice to make. That kiss earlier was so powerful, it took my breath away. I hope he wants to be my mate, but can he handle who I am? It scares me."

Looking in Mel's eyes, I know she sees my worry. "I understand your worry, but I believe that as long as you two waited for each other, everything will work out." Melina is trying to sound convincing. Guess we will find out soon. Standing up, I tell Mel how tired I am and heading to me bed. As I was walking away, I turn back to her because I remembered something she said earlier. I have to ask. "Melina, what is my weakness? You said you know what it is!"

"Well, the Queen Alpha,- you," as she points to me, "the only wolf to have a fated true mate. The rest of us have fated mates, but the two of you are exceptional. That being said, Colt is your weakness, but you are also his. It's probably because you're attached mind, body, and soul. Also, I learned that he is the only Alpha that your Alpha tone doesn't work on!" She burst out laughing holding her stomach. "Poor Colt! I see you two fighting a lot. Both strong-headed, independent Alphas"

"I won't mind the making up, but I figured it was him. Thanks for telling me, Mel. I really need to tell him all of this tomorrow. I love you! Goodnight!" I blow her a kiss and make my way to the cabin.

Walking to my room, I see and smell my mate. Lying on the huge king-size bed with our daughter sleeping in the middle. All I do is take in the sight of my gorgeous mate that I have been blessed with. After a few minutes of gawking, I go to the bathroom and change out of the scrubs into my pjs. I lay on the left side of my daughter. As I am about to fall asleep, I feel a hand touch mine, and it calms me. Opening my eyes to see Colt asleep, but he instinctively reached out to me. We stay like that as I drift off. Thinking about how much I love my mate and connection.

COLT

I wake up at 7:30 a.m. It was the best sleep I have ever had. Looking to see the reason why I slept so well, there she is, lying on her right side, cuddling our daughter, but her left hand is locked in mine. Lying here, I stare at her, seeing the true beauty of my mate. Thinking back to yesterday, I can't believe I didn't feel the bond. What is more perplexing is why do I feel it so much now? She is perfect for me. I couldn't love her more than I do at this moment. It's not just her outer beauty but her inner beauty as well. Thinking about the first time I saw her, I was attracted to her. Maybe subconsciously my wolf was trying to tell me. I don't know, but now my mate and my pups are in our home. From this day I will do whatever it takes to keep her with me. My wolf agrees! I am going to start by making all of them breakfast. Slowly, I let go of her hand and roll out of bed change into a pair of blue shorts and head to the kitchen.

Twenty minutes after I started cooking, Erica, Derrick, and Tyson ask if they can help. Erica and Derrick set the table while Tyson finishes making the eggs and bacon. I start making pancakes, because they are Meadow's favorite. Our first meal as a family, I want to enjoy every minute with them. The boys are going to have to go back to their packs and busy lives.

Without turning around, I knew my mate had entered the room. Her scent was so provocative. I mumble, "Oh, Moon Goddess! You have no idea what she is doing to me, it's killing me! She is driving my wolf and I insane. Every time I smell her scent, I can't concentrate on making these pancakes because of her." Zoey makes her way over to me and touches my bare back. I turn around to her bright green eyes. Her wolf is close to taking over. She moves closer to me. Her hands wander to my back again, as her lips slowly slide to my jaw. I can't help but moan when she bites my earlobe. I didn't realize I leaned down for her to get closer. At that moment, we both catch our breath when she drops her nose to my neck. It's where she will mark me as hers. She is taking in my scent. Turning me hard instantly. I bite my lip, knowing I am about to lose control in front of our pups. "Zoey, you need to stop this now! Our pups are right over there," I whisper, as she lets out a low growl and backs away.

Zoey looks up at me with a devilish grin on her face and replies, "Just so you know, I didn't quit because you used your Alpha command on me. I did it for them," as she points over to the table were Erica, Derrick, Tyson, and Meadow are sitting having a conversation with each other. "Your Alpha tone doesn't work on me, honey." She winks at me and walks over to the table, placing Meadow on her lap, then sits down. As I am finishing the pancakes, in walks Sasha, Sean, Melina, and Chance. Everyone makes their way to the table saying, "It smells so good in here."

No one said a word throughout breakfast, but as we were finishing up, Derrick informs all of us that Erica, Tyson, and him have decided to change their last name. "Mom, we decided that since we know that Colt is our dad, we want to recognize him. We want everyone to know that he is our dad. So, we are going to be known from today as Reese-Westlyn. I want to do this before my pup is born." I am taken aback.

Zoey touches my arm and whispers to me, "Colt, shut your mouth. I know you are in shock, but please close your mouth; no one want to see your food." I look at her, and she winks at me. Closing my mouth, I let out a laugh. Everyone else starts laughing at the situation as well.

"What do you think, Dad? Are you okay with that?" Tyson asks as he looks at me, still laughing. My son just called me Dad for the first time.

"It would be an honor to have my sons take my name. I am also excited for my grandpup to have it!" My sons are incredible young men. I am so overjoyed.

"Mom, Erica and I came up with two names for the pup—a girl name and a boy name. We hope you like them. Erica, tell my mom the names," Derrick announces as he looks at his beautiful mate with nothing but love in his eyes.

"Charlee if it's a girl, and Maximus if it's a boy. What do you think, Zoey?" Erica looks at Zoey for her approval.

My gorgeous mate quickly says, "Why not use both? They are both strong names for my grandpups." As she ends the sentence, her right hand goes to her mouth like she said something she shouldn't have.

"Are you saying that Derrick and I are having twins?" Erica excitedly shrieks.

"I am so sorry to ruin your surprise. I have known for a while. You are going to have healthy, strong twins—a girl and a boy."

"It's okay Zoey! I am glad we found out with our family with us." Erica looks at Derrick, who touches her stomach, then they look at each other with tears of joy in their eyes. It's another emotional moment shared as a family. This first breakfast together is one I will never forget. We are going to have twin grandpups. Everyone congratulates Derrick and Erica. Derrick and Tyson want to spend more time with Meadow, so they go down to the lake. Zoey and I clean up. It gives me alone time with her. I have a question I want to ask her. Finally, when we are done, I turn to her. "Zoey, I want to know if you will go on a date with me this evening? My wolf and I want to get to know our mate. Would you like to go?"

She gives me a megawatt smile and quickly replies, "Of course I do!"

"Well, let's say seven o'clock," I say, and she looks at me.

"Perfect, Colt!"

"I'm sorry, Zoey, but I have work to do in the office for a couple hours. With everything going on, I can't put it off any longer."

"I understand, Colt. I am going to hang out down at the lake with everyone. Meadow is having fun with her brothers and Chance. Just come back when you're done."

I agree and lean in give her kiss on her forehead. "Goodbye, beautiful." Make my way to the door, hoping my mate won't be mad that I just lied to her.

ZOEY

Opening my eyes, I feel a loss. Colt is gone. I understand why I feel the loss. The feeling of holding his hand throughout the night, our connection grew. Lying in bed, thinking of my mate, I am hit with the most alluring scent. MATE! The smell of the ocean and sand. As I am taking in the scent, my daughter decides to wake up. "Mommy, I am hungry!" She looks at me with sand-bags in her eyes.

"Let's go get some breakfast. I think your daddy is making it." She is up and off the bed before I can move. Making my way to the kitchen, I am thunderstruck by the sight of my half-naked mate. Leaning against the door frame, I take him all in. He has his bare back to me, making pancakes with just a pair of blue shorts on. He looks so fucking hot. My wolf is starting to get aroused, and quite frankly, so am I. Striding over to him, I swear I hear him mumbling something to himself. Raising my hand to touch his back sends an incredible shock to my heart. He turns around to look at me, and his eyes are black. His wolf is close to taking over. Without thinking, I lean into him, wanting to feel him closer to me. I wrap my hands around him to his back pulling him closer to me. My lips start dropping little kisses on his jaw. When he lets out a small moan of pleasure, I can't help but bite his earlobe. With that bite, he moves closer to me. I catch my breath when I look to his neck. Wanting to take in my mate's scent, I move to his neck brushing kisses. My wolf's canines were coming out, want-ing to mark our mate.

Colt snaps me out of it when he says, "Zoey, you need to stop this now. Our pups are right over there." I let out a low growl and back away from him. My wolf is thinking dirty thoughts of our mate. I give him a devilish grin, letting him know I want to complete the mating bond. "Just so you know, I didn't quit because you used your Alpha command on me. I did it for them," as I point at our pups. "Your Alpha tone doesn't work on me, honey." I wink at him and walk over to the table where my pups are sitting talking to each other. When I sit down at the table, I place Meadow on my lap, trying not to focus on Colt. Sasha, Sean, Melina, and Chance walk into the kitchen saying something smells good. Thank the Moon Goddess they have perfect timing.

We all sat through breakfast in silence. Wolves love to eat. Eating is no joke for us. We eat till it's all gone. Shifting takes a lot of energy, so eating keeps our strength up. As we are finishing, Derrick informs us that Erica, Tyson, and him decided to change their last names. Melina mindlinks me during Derrick's conversation. "Derrick and I had a talk last night after you went to bed. He and Tyson want everyone to know the Colt is their dad. So, I gave him the idea about the name change. I hope you're not upset with me."

Smiling at her, I reply, "Not at all. One of the many reasons you are going to make an incredible 'right hand.' Thank you for giving Derrick great advice."

"Colt, shut your mouth. I know you are in shock, but please close your mouth; no one wants to see your food." I wink at him, and everyone laughs.

Tyson asks what Colt thinks. Colt is happy with the news but especially excited that he is going to be a granddad. Derrick then changes the subject to the baby names. They have finally decided. Erica looks to me and says, "Charlee if it's a girl, and Maximus if it's a boy. What do you think, Zoey?" Erica sees the smile on my face.

Without thinking, I say, "Why not use both? They are both strong names for my grandpups." As soon as I say it, I put my right hand over my mouth. I shouldn't have said anything to anyone. I have known from the beginning. Before Erica told anyone she was pregnant, I already knew she was. Her scent changed. The first time I touched her stomach, I felt two heartbeats, and then I had a vision before I came here that involved a little girl and boy.

"Are you saying that Derrick and I are having twins?" Erica's voice is high pitched with excitement.

"I am so sorry to ruin the surprise. I got caught up in the moment, but I have known for a while. You are going to have healthy, strong twins—one boy and one girl."

"It's okay, Zoey! We are glad we found out with our family." Erica looks to my son, who touches her stomach, it's a moment I will never forget. My son has tears of joy in his eyes, and so does everyone else. These two are going to phenomenal parents. I am so excited to be a Ya-Ya! The name means a lot to Derrick when he was a pup. His teddy bear, Ya-Ya, gave him security and comfort. That's what I want to be for my grandpups. Also, I kept his Ya-Ya tucked away and plan to give it to them when the twins arrive. Everyone is congratulating Erica and Derrick when Meadow jumps down off my lap and walks over to Tyson. She asks him to take her down to the lake. Derrick and Tyson look to me and say that they will take her down because they want to spend time with her. Sasha, Sean, Melina, and Chance decide to go with them on this beautiful morning.

Colt and I stay behind to clean up. He is nervous, I can feel it. When we finish, he turns to me. "Zoey, I would like to take you on a date this evening. My wolf and I want to spend time getting to know our mate. Will you do me the honor of being my date tonight?"

I beam at him with excitement. "Of course I do."

"Well, let's say seven o'clock." He is grinning back at me. "I'm sorry, Zoey, but I have work to do in the office for a couple hours. With everything going on, I have to catch up on paperwork. I can't put it off any longer," he calmly explains to me.

"I understand, Colt." He is lying to me, but I let it go. He still doesn't understand who I am. "I am going to hang out at the lake with everyone. Meadow is so happy spending time with her brothers and Chance. Just come back when you're done."

Leaning in, he kissed my forehead. "Goodbye, beautiful," turning away and walking out the door. I let out a little chuckle knowing what he is up to but feeling uneasy that he lied to me. "He wants to surprise us, Zoey." My wolf keeps screaming in my head. I let it go because I have more important things to worry about. What am I going to wear tonight?

COLT

It took me all afternoon to get everything ready for our date. I want it to be perfect for her. Showing up at the cabin in dark blue dress shorts with a light blue button-up short-sleeve dress shirt. Zoey answers the door in a hunter-green off-the-shoulder mid-length sundress; my eyes go straight to her breasts. They look gigantic in that dress. "My eyes are up here." She smirks at me. I hand her bouquet of daisies, her favorite, I picked for her. Our hands touch; the sparks and electricity are overwhelming. How am I going to get through tonight without claiming her? She walks over to the kitchen counter and sets the flowers down. Making her way back to me, I take in how breathtakingly beautiful she is. I take her hand in my mine, relishing her touch. We head to the eastern part of the packlands. Walking was definitely a great idea. We talk about her practice, the boys, Meadow, and about the dreams I had about her. When we walk through the tree line, Zoey gasps. I know she loves the view before her. The moon is reflecting off the huge lake and waterfall. A table for two is sitting beside the lake. I have candles burning with soft music playing in the background. I have to pat myself on the back for choosing such a romantic spot. I have never been the romantic type, but for her it comes so easy. The woman is nothing I ever dreamed of as a mate. She is so much more. I still feel terrible that I didn't recognize her as my mate. She keeps saying it was the spell, but it's still a tough pill to swallow. Guiding her over to the table, I pull out her chair, and as she sits down, I lean down to her neck to take in her scent. After a couple seconds, I make my way over to the chair and sit across from her with a smirk on my face. One of our young pack warriors brings our food to us. As he lifts the lids, she looks to me. "You made New York strip, mashed potatoes, and Brussel sprouts. How did you know that is my favorite meal?"

I snort and inform her I had help from Melina.

"Dinner was amazing, Colt! Thank you! I didn't know you could cook." She looks so beautiful in the moonlight.

"I can grill and make pancakes, but truth be told, I had a lot of help to get this done today. I don't like lying to you, even about the small stuff."

She is watching me intently. "I was mad at first, but I figured and my wolf convinced me you had a good reason. Remember who I am, Colt. I can always tell when someone is lying to me. Now that being said, whoever helped you today, thank them; they did an amazing job. This is absolutely beautiful." She looks around in awe.

"Zoey, I want to ask you a question. Are you glad that I am your mate?"

She responds quickly, "Of course, Colt! From the day I saw you, my wolf screamed mate! It was the most amazing day of my life. I was looking at my other half for what seems like forever. The one the Moon Goddess chose for me, but when you didn't recognize me, it made me more determined to find out why. I don't blame you at all, so please don't blame yourself. Do you feel the bond now?" She looks at me like she is scared to hear my answer.

"Of course I do! I waited so long for you. You, my love, are all my dreams come true. I never want this feeling to end." Taking her hand while looking her in the eyes with all my love so she sees the truth.

"Colt, do you want to take over as Alpha when your dad retires? Or do you want to stay here if you don't?" She is worried I am going to reject her. I can feel all her emotions.

"Yes, Zoey, I do want to be Alpha of this pack. It is mine to inherit. If you don't want me to take over, I won't. Being with you is more important than being Alpha. I hope you know that. But I have been dreaming of taking over with my mate, my Luna, beside me to lead this amazing pack. I love it here. Tell me you will stay here with me and help me rule the pack?" trying not to sound needy, but in reality, I need her to stand beside me. The bond that we share is so important to an Alpha.

"Colt, I would never ask you to give up being Alpha. I will stand beside you in whatever you decide. Just understand that being Queen Alpha, I will travel to other packs because they need my guidance just as much as this pack." Zoey seems to question if I can do both.

"As Alpha, I will have a strong Beta and Gamma to help me. Zoey, you won't have to worry about anything. I thought this entire situation out already. I promise!" trying to calm her fears. Because I can feel her nerves. It's like she has something to tell me but is afraid to say it out loud.

"We have waited for a long time to find each other. Thank the Moon Goddess for not giving up on us and finally bringing us together. From the first day I saw you, you had my heart and soul. It was an immediate bond. Then I look into your eyes, and I see the future we will have together. You are my one and only, Colt! I want to share my entire life with you. But I must ask, what do you want, and can you handle me as Queen Alpha?" There it is. The real reason she is scared. Zoey thinks I don't want her or am having second thoughts. I need her to know what I feel for her is more than she can imagine.

"Sweetheart, I may not of felt your bond in the beginning, but I feel it now. My heart only beats for you. I feel a loss when I am not with you. The fire and sparks when you touch me drive me crazy. Don't ever question my love for you. It's never-ending. As for you being the Queen Alpha, I find it sexy as hell that you are strong and independent; you can take care of yourself, but I will always have your back. It's a really nice view." I wink, and she blushes. She can feel I am speaking to her with love and honesty. I am one lucky man and wolf to have her as my mate. Without another word, I stand up and go to her. Leaning down, I place my palm to her cheek. The fire within me ignites again. When I lean in closer, my lips are moving to hers. Once again, I feel passion and electricity flow through my body. Zoey bites my bottom lip and I growl with excitement. I need her as much as she wants me.

Slowly, she stands up from the table and looks at me with glassy, bright-green eyes. And asks, "Can I see your wolf? I haven't seen him, and my wolf wants to see him so badly."

"Of course, baby! I thought you would never ask; my wolf is driving me insane. He wants to make sure she is okay. Go over by one of the trees and undress meet me right back here when you are ready, okay?" Zoey nods and begins make her way over to a huge oak tree to strip. My wolf and I are giddy with excitement to see her wolf again. We both agree that our mate is stunning, ravishing, exquisite, angelic, and the sexist human and wolf we have ever laid eyes on. I hurry to strip off my cloths and shift into my wolf, anticipating the arrival of our other half. When she appears, I am blown away. Her wolf is staring at us like she is going to fuck us seven shades from Sunday. My wolf drops his two front paws to the ground and bows his head to her. We let her know that we both accept her as our Queen. She leans in and nuzzles her head to mine. Sounding like purring coming from her. Then she sits back on her hind legs and stares at me in wolf form. It's her turn to take me in. Not long after, she struts back behind the tree to shift and change back into her clothes. I do the same. Standing by the lake, watching the moon sparkle into the water. Zoey surprises me by touching my shoulder. Turning to look at her, no words said, I lean in for another kiss. I will never get tired of her soft lips on mine. We slowly move and sit down in the sand, looking out at the water in complete silence. Now this is how I would love to end my days with her.

After a few minutes, Zoey breaks the silence. She leans in and puts her head on my shoulder. The more our bond grows, the more I can feel her emotions. I know she has more on her mind. "Zoey, what's bothering you?"

Still looking at the water, she replies, "How do you know that something is bothering me?"

"I can feel your emotions more with our bond getting stronger. Please tell me!"

Suddenly she starts whispering, "Melina went back to our pack to do the DNA test. She came across a book. Inside the book had two words: Queen Alpha. My sister has always been an inquisitive person, so she read it and informed me last night what was written in the book. It described my powers, my mate's powers, our mating ceremony, and even my family's bloodline."

"So is that what you needed to talk to her about last night?"

"It wasn't, but what Melina told me ended up coming back to what her and I needed to discuss. She informed me that my family, the Westlyns, are purebloods. That our pups will have gifts just like you and me. The Moon Goddess chose me to be Queen. Did you know that the first Queen came to be around four thousand years ago? She is the only Queen to be accepted by her mate. I guess the other mates couldn't accept the power a Queen possesses. Her and her fated true mate are the most beloved and powerful of our kind, but other species fear us. Melina mentioned you and I will come into some of our powers when we consummate our relationship, claiming each other both sexually and marking. At my coronation, our powers will be completely gifted to us by the Moon Goddess. She'll gift them to us for our love, commitment, and bond we have to our kind. It didn't really mention what your power will be."

I cut her off. "I will be your protector. I remembered yesterday the stories my dad told us when we were pups. Not ever thinking it would be me. The protector will be a master of strength, combat, and weapons. Your protector, me, will protect you with my life, Zoey. I will always protect you. You have my solemn vow." She sighed, never moving her head from my shoulder, but her eyes lifted to mines. I could see her love for me gazing right into my soul.

Without blinking, she calmly spoke, "I figured you might have an idea. Because I knew most of the information she told me. It's weird how I just know. Mel brought up our mating ceremony. We have a forty-eight-hour window to mate, or our bond will sever. Neither one of us will get a second-chance mate. If we mate, truly become one, we will be of one mind, body, and soul. Our bloodline will be the strongest of our kind. Our heirs are going to be powerful and receive their powers when I receive all mine.

They will be immune to silver and wolfsbane like us. That reminds me, just so you know, that's how I healed so quick after the explosion. My body just needed to recuperate."

"Thank you for telling me everything, baby. It's a lot to take in. Please never fear telling me anything. I want a relationship with you that is open and honest." Turning my body to have her full attention, "Let's have the mating ceremony tomorrow evening. We don't want to waste anymore precious time without each other. We have waited long enough. I want everyone to know you are mine! I love you, Zoey Westlyn, with my entire heart." Tears are slowly rolling down her cheeks and I brush them away with my thumb.

"I love you, Colt! I loved you from the moment I first saw you." I have to lean in and kiss this woman who has become my entire world in a short period of time. So, this is what true love feels like. Thank you, Moon Goddess, for this incredible gift.

After a brief make-out session in the sand, Zoey stops to tell me two other things she talked to Melina about last night. "Mel told me as Queen I have one weakness." Taking her hand in mine.

"It's me!" It comes out of my mouth without thinking.

"Yes, you are my weakness, but I am also yours." Did she think that would change my mind about taking her as my mate?

"Baby, you are my weakness, and I didn't need a book to tell me. I am not surprised by this at all." Truthfully, I am not shocked. We have a connection to one another that is different from anyone else.

"It's unbreakable!" my wolf says. "We will just keep each other close. I kind of like having you near me. It calms me and my wolf."

Zoey leans over and kisses my lips so softly and says, "I couldn't of ask for a better protector, man, and mate; thank you for accepting all of me." This woman is thanking me when I should be thanking her. Just means we are meant and destined for each other. Pulling her close to me, I ask if she is ready for bed; it's getting late. "Yes!" as she yawns. We make our way back to the cabin. "Do you want to stay with me tonight, Colt?" looking at me with little wolf eyes.

"I would love to, baby, but I have a lot to prepare for tomorrow. And I really do have pack business to attend to." She knows I am telling her the truth. Yawning again, I bend down and kiss my mate on the forehead. "Goodnight, my love! I will see you tomorrow for our mating ceremony. I love you, Zoey!

"I love you, Colt. Goodnight!" turning around to close the door and turn off the living room light.

ZOEY

Waking up early, I am so excited that today I will finally be mated to my fated true mate. He left a note to take the girls to the mall to get dresses and whatever else I need for today. Getting Melina, Cara, Sasha, Erica, and Meadow moving is a chore, to say it politely. When we are ready to leave, I see my boys, Sean, Nico, and Chance, piling into Derrick's car. I know they are heading to the packhouse. We all wave at them as they pull out. Mel, Erica, Meadow, and I jump into Mel's SUV, while Sasha rides with Cara. Pulling into the mall, it's nine a.m. The stores are just opening. Cole texts me.

"Our mating ceremony is set for five p.m. at the cabin. You and the girls have fun and take your time. I am taking care of everything. Enjoy your day. I love you so much, Zoey! Today is the happiest day of my life."

I start to cry happy tears as I re-read his message. I never thought this day would come. Feeling so blessed and thankful, I make my way into David's Bridal. An older lady in her late sixties with short, grey hair makes her way over to me. We inform her that we need the dresses for today; she almost faints. She's also human.

"We have our work cut out for us; you are going to be limited to what we have available in the store." I tell her that we understand the situation politely as I can. Mel, Erica, and Sasha are trying on dresses while Meadow, Cara, and I go look for shoes. We happen to pass a nail and hair salon. Quickly, I make appointments for all of us at noon and one p.m.

Cara and I are looking at shoes, and she looks at me. "I have never seen my brother so happy. None of us ever liked Stefanie, and I am so glad he didn't settle. Zoey, I am so honored to be in your mating ceremony. Standing with you as you claim your mate for life, who happens to be my big brother, is a special occasion. Thank you for seeing what a wonderful man he is. I am so excited to have you as my sister," pulling me in for a hug. We finish picking out our shoes and head back to the bridal shop.

As we enter, Mel looks at me with a big smile on her face. "Did you find what you were looking for?"

"I found these six-inch heels with diamonds on them. What do you think?" pulling them out of the box. "I need all the height to stand next to Colt." She rolls her eyes, knowing I am right.

"Well, I found my dress; now it's your turn, Zoey. Go look over there and tell the attendant what you are looking for. She is really good at her job. She picked me out a purple, ruffle off-the-shoulder mini dress that I love." She unzips the bag to show me. It's exactly what I would pick for her. It's beautiful. As we finish, in walks Vixen. She is always late. She had a call from our pack, and she had to deal with a medical crisis. My sister is the only one that found her fated mate. Well, not after today. She hugs Mel and I and makes her way to the dresses. I know she is happy for me. We are all close, but I can feel her worry for me. Of all of us, she is the worrier.

Looking back to Mel, "I need to ask you an important question. Since this is kind of like a marriage, I would like you to be what humans call a maid of honor? I need you beside me."

She draws me in for a tight squeeze. "I wouldn't be anywhere else. I will always stand beside you. Thank you for asking me. I am so excited for you. Finally finding your fated true mate and your happily ever after."

"Thank you! I can't believe it is happening so fast." Giddiness takes over. I make my way over to the dresses and Mel leaves to look for shoes to match her dress.

After an hour of trying on dresses, I find the perfect dress. A white spaghetti-strap split-front lace beach dress. My curves and boobs pop. Colt will lose his mind when he sees me in this. Now that I found my dress, I turn the Meadow. "It's your turn, princess."

She grins up at me and says, "I found my dress, Mommy. It

looks like yours. I want to look like you today."

As I turn to see a young attendant, a she-wolf, coming through the side door with a small dress that looks almost like mine. "She tried it on already. She was watching you try on yours so I went in the back and found this one. She really loves you, my Queen."

"Thank you for this. I appreciate it so much."

She bows her head and turns away.

The other attendant speaks up. "We can send all the dresses and shoes to your house after we fix the two dresses that need hemmed. No extra charge. Enjoy your wedding day, madam." I guess that is what humans call our mating ceremony. Except we mate for life. There is no chance for divorce. "Anything I can do to help our future Alpha and Luna, please let me know. My name is Reba." The helpful she-wolf chimes in.

"Thank you for all you help." I turn and head to get my hair done.

Over the next couple of hours the girls and I are pampered. Laughing and carry on. It's a memorable occasion for all of us. Meadow loved being treated like a true princess. She had the works with hair and nails. Sitting watching her get an updo just like me, I start to get sentimental. My heart is full of joy!

By the time we are all done and arrive home at the cabin, it looks completely unrecognizable. A huge arch is right on the beach with beautiful arrangements of pink, green, yellow, peach, purple, and white flowers everywhere. About one hundred chairs covered in white cloth. A beautiful, glittery runway leading from the cabin to the arch. Colt has large white lights hanging. The DJ is setting up by the firepit. I look to my left and see twenty tables with white tablecloths, candles, and flowers covering them all. It's absolutely gorgeous. My mate has really outdone himself. He thought of everything. The pack did an incredible job making this perfect. Melina is the first say, "Zoey, your mate made this look like Paradise Island. It's stunning. I am so happy for you and a little jealous." I know she is happy for me, but I see the tears in her eyes. Sadness for herself. The other girls walk over and gush over my mate's decorating skills. We make our way into the cabin; to our surprise, our gowns are hanging in the living room. Looking to the clock, it's almost four o'clock; the guests will be arriving soon. Everyone starts to do their make-up and get dressed. As I finish getting my dress on, I hear a knock on the door to my bedroom.

"Come in!"

The door opens to my parents. Seeing me in my dress, both of them get choked up. My daddy is trying to be a strong Alpha but failing miserably. "Zoey, you look stunning. I am so happy that you finally found your mate. Colt is a good man. He is very lucky to have you as a mate." The tears start rolling as we embrace each other.

"Thanks, Daddy! But you are biased when it comes to Colt and me. Colt and I are lucky that the Moon Goddess blessed us with each other." My dad agrees with me as I look over to my mom.

"My daughter is having her mating ceremony. I wished for it so long, and now it's here. I love you, Zoey, and we wish you both a long and blessed life together. You both deserve happiness." She is starting to sob.

Taking her hand. "I just want what you and Daddy have. Looking up to you two my entire life. If Colt and I are half as lucky as you two are, we will be blessed." Now we are both sobbing. My parents leave and fix my make-up. The music starts to play. Exiting my room, I see girls in the living room waiting for me. They all gasp when they see me. Erica is the first to say I look exquisite. Sasha and Cara say I look radiant. Mel says drop-dead gorgeous. When I turn to the kitchen, I see Meadow. She looks like an angel.

"You look like a true princess today, sweetie," bending down to give my daughter a hug.

"Thank you, Mommy! You look like a Queen. Daddy is going to faint when he sees you." She has her daddy's smile.

My dad walks into the cabin and says, "It's showtime, ladies!" The girls decided to get the same dress as Melina but in different colors. Vixen is the first to step to the door. She turns to me smiles and winks, then makes her way outside in her hot-pink dress. Of the three of us, she has always been the colorful one. Her office walls back home are hot pink. Cara is the one to make her way to the doorway; she turns to me. "Catie feels terrible that her and Gage couldn't be here. Gage's grandmother is doing better today; she told me when she called earlier. She wanted you to know how happy she is for you and Colt," turning to leave in her light-blue dress. It makes her blue eyes pop.

Sasha hugs me, then walks out the door in her light-peach dress; she should wear the color more often because she looks breathtaking in it with her dark hair.

Erica is the next one to go. She stops and looks at me. "Derrick and I are so happy for you and Colt. Thank you for being an awesome mom to my mate. I love you!" She winks and walks out the door. That young woman was made for my son. He is a lucky man. I just adore her.

My mini-me is standing in the doorway. "Mommy, I will be waiting for you beside Daddy and Chance. You're beautiful." She turns back to see Chance waiting for her. They make their way down together, dropping her petals along the way.

Mel is standing at the door frame, staring straight ahead. I can feel her sadness. "Mel, what's wrong? Are you okay?"

She turns to me. "Just know this, I really love you to do this today." She gives me an evil glare, and then she is gone.

"You ready, Zoey!" My dad draws me back.

"Wait a minute." I give him a smirk.

The DJ announces, "The Queen requested this song to walk to her mate. She also wants everyone here to know that she sang this song to him once, and today he will become all mine! Without further ado." The song starts to play, "The Good Ones" by Gabby Barrett. It's one of my favorite songs and fitting for our mating ceremony. As I make my way out of the cabin on my daddy's arm, all I can see is Colt. Never seeing all the guests. All I could see is my mate. In his white short-sleeve shirt and tan dress shorts. His short dark-as-night hair and ocean-blue eyes looking into my soul. I am blown away by the intensity in his eyes. He is smoking hot, my wolf comments. Looking him up and down taking every part of him in, I notice he is barefoot in the sand.

COLT

The pack members did exactly what I ask of them. It's stunning! The cabin has been turned into the paradise Zoey deserves. Twenty minutes before the ceremony, Alpha Zane and my dad pull me aside. My dad is the first speak. "Colt, we want to talk to you before your mating ceremony." I look at them, unsure what this is about. Then my dad continues with a smirk on his face. "Colt, don't worry, it's not bad. As your dad I wanted to congratulate you and Zoey on finally finding each other. She is a beautiful, kind woman. The Moon Goddess made a wise choice pairing the two of you. I just want to give you some fatherly advice…. Love your mate without end. Be her foundation and her heart. She needs you as much as you need her. Both of you are strong Alphas, so always treat her as your equal. Zoey is going to be an unbelievable Queen. Always be there for her. I love you! Again, congratulations, son!" He gives me a big bear hug. He is trying not to show his emotions. I know he is so thrilled about Zoey being my mate. As dad pulls away, Alpha Zane gives me an amused look.

"My turn," Zane says looking me straight into the eyes. "Your dad and I will always be here for you. We know how difficult your mate can be." They laugh and roll their eyes. "Just love her, support her, be honest with her, and protect her. She is going to need you to help her handle the enormous amount of powers she is going to blessed with. We are looking forward to seeing the two of you ruling together. Welcome to our family, Colt. I couldn't have picked a better mate for my daughter." When Zane finishes, I am speechless. , I extend my hand to shake my soon-to-be-father's hand, but he gives me a bear hug instead. "Keep our girl safe," he whispers with tenderness in his voice. There is no doubt how much he loves his daughter.

The Moon Goddess graced us a beautiful day for our mating ceremony. Looking out at the pack members and family here to celebrate with us is heartwarming. Everyone is cheery and joyous for us. Turning to my left, I look at my wedding council. Chase is what humans call a best man. He looks a little rattled, staring at the cabin, not saying a word. Next to him stands Derrick, Tyson, Sean, and Nico. They are joking around with one another. The music starts to play, and one by one the ladies make their way down the aisle Vixen is the first to walk out. She looks at Nico with a mega smile on her face. Cara is slowly walking out, but she is shyly looking at my dad. Then she looks straight ahead, ignoring me and the guys. Why? Sasha is next, blushing while looking at my dad. When I look at my dad, he looks at me and smiles. "We will talk later!" he mindlinks me. I nod. What the hell is wrong with my family today? Erica is the next to make her way down the aisle. Her baby bump is obvious in this dress. She winks to both Derrick and me. My son is a blessed man. I turn and look to him and see a younger me. I look to see Meadow with Chance. She looks like a princess in her dress. She is lovely walking down, dropping her flower petals along the way. They both stand in front of me and Chase.

Meadow and Chase turn and say in unison, "She is beautiful; you're going to faint!" Chase hits me on the arm and laughs out loud. His laughter stops suddenly when he looks to the cabin to see Melina walking toward us. Melina doesn't look happy 'til she glances at Chance, then her whole demeanor changes. There is no doubt that she loves and adores her son. A low growl comes from Chase, and I elbow him in his ribs, holding his stare on Melina as she comes to her place standing across from us. Melina never looks our way. She just turns to the DJ as he starts to speak. He explains that Zoey picked this song to walk to me. I get excited. The song starts, and I know exactly why she chose this song. From this day forward, she will be mine and I will be hers. When she walks out of the cabin, she takes me breath away. Her beauty catches me off guard. Today, she looks like an angel. My Queen!

I can't take my eyes off her. I love this woman completely.

Alpha Zane and Zoey are standing in front of me, and she hasn't taken her eyes off me since she walked out of the cabin. I am awestruck again when she gives me that megawatt smile. No woman will ever compare to my mate. Zane kisses her on the cheek and makes his way over to sit beside Violet. Zoey ask Alpha Knox to be the master of ceremonies for our day.

Knox clears his throat. "We are gathered here today to witness the mating of these two fated true mates. Moments ago, I was also informed by Alpha Craig that this will be Colt's Alpha ceremony along with Zoey's oath as Luna." Everyone gasps in surprise. I turn and look at my dad.

"It's your time to take over. I have no doubt the two of you will do unbelievable things not only for this pack but all our packs," my dad expresses to both Zoey and I. "That being said, we will start with the mating ceremony. Zoey and Colt decided to write their own declaration to one another. Zoey, why don't you go first." Knox looks to her and she hands her flowers to Melina. She turns to face me, placing her hands in mine.

"Colt, from the time I was a young pup I couldn't wait to find my other half. We waited for a long time to find each other, but you were worth the wait. The Moon Goddess picked the perfect man to be my mate. From the day you jumped out of that truck, you had my heart. I felt the connection to you immediately; you are the father to our pups, my mate, my best friend, my protector, and my Alpha. As I stand here today, I couldn't of ask for anyone better to spend my life with. I promise to be a loving Luna to this pack. I promise to be a loving and faithful mate. Most importantly, I promise to love you with my entire heart for the rest of my life. Every day I will be grateful to the Moon Goddess that she blessed me with you. Today we begin our lives together, and I can't wait. I love you, Colt! Now and forever!" Beaming up at me, I could see all her love for me in her eyes.

"That was beautiful, Zoey," Knox says as he looks over to me.

"Zoey, when I felt the bond, it came strong, fast, and hard. I have no doubt that we will rule this pack and the other three with strength, love, and compassion. I promise you that as long I breathe, you will never be alone. I promise to tell you every day how beautiful you are. I never want you to question that. You're my best friend, my mate, my Luna, and my Queen always and forever. I believe I was brought into this world to be loved by you and you were brought into this world to be cherished by me. I am looking forward to our future together. I love you, Zoey!"

Tears are running down Zoey's face. "I didn't think I could love you anymore than I do, but you say all those beautiful words...I love you more and more every day." She kisses my hands. Knox takes the mating knife out of his back pocket. We both lift our left hands. I know Zoey hates this part. Knox cuts both our palms, and neither of us move a muscle. We just look into each other's eyes. Placing our hands together, wrapping them with the sacred cloth of our pack colors. As soon as he starts, I can feel the power enter my body. Feeling the connection to Zoey even more. Knox says, "Dear Moon Goddess, bless this mating; give them a long and happy life together. We stand witness to the bond you have created. Bless them today and forever. May their love last forever without end." I felt us become one. Feeling complete, I look down at our palms, which are already healed. Knox is holding the cloth in his hands, smiling at Zoey. When I look to Zoey, her eyes are ablaze. Staring at me for the first time, I feel the bond to my sons. Our family is complete. Turning to them, I see that their eyes are also glowing. Looking down at Meadow, her eyes are also aglow.

Glancing back to my mate, I hear, "Colt, please don't look at me like that or I will fuck you right here."

Grinning ear to ear at her. "I can hear you, baby!" Her eyes go wide and she blushes crimson.

"Really!" she whispers to me.

"Yes! And I feel the same way, so stop looking at me with those 'fuck me' eyes!" this time I mindlink her.

"Okay! I heard you. I can't believe how fast that happen." She's still blushing and maybe a little overwhelmed by the quickness of our bond.

"Craig, can you come up here, please?" Knox breaks our mindlink. My dad makes his way over to us. Zoey moves to stand beside me with a smirk on her face. I love being the reason she smiles. "MINE!" my wolf keeps saying.

My dad starts, "Colt, the time has come for you take your place of the Alpha of the Reese pack. Do you promise to lead, protect, and defend this pack to the best of your ability?"

"I promise!" completely meaning it.

"Do you accept the role as Alpha of the Reese pack?"

"I accept!" As soon as the words leave my mouth, I am overcome again with power. Feeling the strength and honor of being an Alpha. The bond to everyone in my pack is so strong. My dad looks to Zoey. "Zoey Reese, do you accept the Reese pack as your pack from this day forward?" My dad looks at her lovingly.

"I do!" Zoey respectfully replies.

"Do you promise to lead this pack with love, compassion and honor?"

"I promise!" she affectionately answers.

"Do you accept the role as Luna of the Reese pack?"

"I accept!" she beams up at me.

Everyone applauds and cheers. My dad bends down to hug Zoey and then me. "Daisy would be so proud today. We have loved Zoey since she was born. Today, my goddaughter became our daughter and Luna. I love you both! Always look to each other if you need help. You're a team. Remember that!"

"Thanks, Dad!" I say, knowing he had to do both jobs most of his reign as Alpha. It's finally his time to relax and enjoy his life. Zoey hugs him tight. When she steps back, she winks at him; did she just mindlink my dad? What was that about?

I look to my mate, my Luna and soon to be Queen to all wolves. All I can do is lean in and kiss her soft lips. When we pull back from the breathtaking first kiss as mates, we both say, "MINE!" Our wolves are starting to get horny. "Yours always and forever," Zoey says in a sweet and loving tone. We make our way over to our table while the DJ plays soft dinner music. We are finishing up dinner when Zoey stands up, surprising me.

"Thank you all for coming today on such short notice. This has been an incredible day for us. I am blessed to be a member of this pack and have Colt as our Alpha. I am proud to be his mate and Luna. I promise to always do my best for each and every one of you. Please raise a glass to my mate and Alpha. May he lead with courage, honor, and compassion. May he always be the best of our pack. To our strong and warrior Alpha, may the Moon Goddess keep you safe from harm." As Zoey raises her glass, so does everyone else. This woman does and says things that leave me awestruck. Her confidence in me is unwavering. I stand up and grab her for the most passionate kiss. I love and respect her so much. Pulling back from our kiss, she is surprised. Good! Glad I can shock her as well.

Before we know it, it's time for us to leave. We make out way around the pack members and family telling them thank you for attending. Melina is the last person we stop to talk too. She has been bugging us about where we are going. I keep telling her it's a "surprise!"

"I am so happy for you both. Colt, take care of my sister and our Queen." Melina looks to us both.

"I promise!" I grin, looking at my beautiful mate. My wolf and I are so excited and desperate to have her alone. Melina pulls me aside, out of Zoey's hearing so she talk. "Just so you know, Zoey won't tell you but she has read the *Fifty Shades* trilogy over a hundred times. She may be a virgin, but she knows what she wants." Melina winks to me.

"Okay! TMI, Melina!" I yell but blush from her oversharing.

"I'm just trying to help my sister out." She bows her head to me and walks away. I make my way to my mate, taking her hand and heading to our special place.

ZOEY

Walking toward the lake hand in hand, I am lost in him. His scent is consuming. He apparently has been talking to me and I didn't hear a word. "Sorry, I missed what you said." He laughs, knowing why I didn't hear him. He smells my arousal.

"Follow me closely. When I was a pup, I found this special place. I never shared it with anyone, but today I want it to be ours," Colt says, as he rubs his thumb over my hand trying to calm each other down. Releasing my hand, he walks in front of me. He leads me toward the huge boulders by the waterfall. What is he doing so close to the water? Using his Alpha strength, he moves the large boulder to the side with ease. He steps aside and lets me enter an opening on the other side of the waterfall. Taking my hand back into his, leading me in looking to my left, the waterfall looks like a wall of water. I am impressed by the beauty of the misting waterfall. Apparently, I was so awestruck that I didn't notice to the right of me is a king-size bed covered in emerald-green satin sheets. The small cave has around a hundred candles placed throughout. It's perfect. Just like my mate. After taking it all in, I look to Colt, who is trying to read my reaction. "Thank you for sharing this with me. It is stunning."

"Not as beautiful as you, my love," he says as he runs his thumb over my bottom lip. Before I can respond to him, he pulls me in to a kiss that has so much want and passion. Feeling the thirst building within me, I put both my hands into his dark hair, pulling him closer to me, deepening our kiss. Colt groans, then picks me up and walks us to the bed. He lays me carefully on the cool, silky sheets like I am delicate china. He leans back with a sexy-as-fuck stare and starts to undress me. Starting with my high heels, softly kissing up my leg into my inner thigh. I hear him taking a deep breath. Wanting to take in my scent, I lie just looking at my hot mate, making me feel fire and tingle throughout my body. He is the hottest man I have ever seen. Suddenly he stops, looks up to me with lust in his eyes. Before I can do anything, he is hovering over me. Carefully, he pulls my straps down on my mating dress. His touch starts to make me squirm. It's magical. I am starting to overheat. Colt gasps when he realizes that I am completely nude under my dress. "You're the sexiest woman alive. I can't wait much longer to be inside you." It's almost breathless, but he continues to stare at my naked body, taking me in. I love that I can do this to my mate. Feeling his loss as soon as he stands up and starts to undress. As he takes off his shirt, pants, and boxers, he never takes his eyes off of me. Now it's my turn to take all of him in. He's fucking built. I am intoxicated by his smell. His cock is so hard, fucking enormous. He crawls back onto the bed between my legs; leaning down, Colt starts to give me soft butterfly kisses in my inner thigh 'til he reaches his goal. Starting to lick my clit, I arch my back off the bed and moan in ecstasy. When he starts to finger me, I moan even louder. An orgasm is building when he abruptly stops. "Baby, you're so tight and I need to have you right now," almost growling it out. His wolf is close to the surface. "Our first time together, we are going to climax together." He licks his fingers as drifts overtop of me. Looking me in the eyes with lust, he says, "This may hurt for a little, but tell me if it's too painful and I will stop. I never want to hurt you." He kisses me forehead and continues, "You are my dreams come true, my world, my queen, you own me mind, body, and soul."

As he finishes, I feel a sharp pain. I gasp and close my eyes, taking him all in, no longer a virgin. Colt stays still, feeling him watching me carefully. The pain starts to subside. I look back into his worried eyes and say, "Move, Colt! I need you so much right now." Slowly, he starts to move, but I feel the building again. I scream, "Faster, harder, please!" doing exactly what I ask. Slamming into me hitting my sweet spot. Without realizing it, I am sitting on him, and we are face-to-face. Intensely staring into my soul. An orgasm in building up with more passion in this position. "Baby, my wolf and I want to mark you. I can't hold him back any longer." Pulling myself closer to him, I take control, riding him. Colt starts to kiss my neck, feeling his fangs at my neck with need to claim me as his. I follow his lead and do the same thing. We bite down at the same time, marking each other, causing us both an unimaginable first orgasm together. It hits so fast and hard. My wolf feels serene. We both lick each other's necks to clean our wounds. No words can express the feeling to with my fated true mate now that our bond is complete. I am over-whelmed by love, peace, and complete. My other half is finally home. Colt lays me back onto the mattress and gets up walks over to the waterfall. When he returns, he has a wet towel and starts cleaning me up; when I look down, I see and smell blood.

"It's okay, Zoey! As your mate I will always take care of you first. Just rest, baby." Calmly speaking to me. A few seconds later, I feel the bed dip and feel his arms wrap around me, pulling me to him. My back to his front, he whispers into my ear, "Forever yours. I love you, Zoey!"

"Mine! Always and forever. I love you, Colt," saying as I fall into the most relaxing and content sleep of my life.

Waking up in the middle of the night with the urge to pee, completely naked, I realize I have to walk outside the cave to do my business. Coming back into our "paradise," I pass a huge eight-foot mirror catching my reflection of my left side of my neck. Walking closer, right where Colt marked me I see a crown with Colt underneath it. My wolf is so thrilled that everyone will know that I am forever his. Thank you, Moon Goddess, for never giving up on us. He is truly an incredible man and wolf. Making my way back to bed, I see Colt's neck. He has his head turned to the right making his left side of his neck visible to me. My mark on him, a crown with Zoey underneath it, making me and my wolf overjoyed. "Mine forever," my wolf yells. Without waking up, Colt pulls me to him, laying my head on his chest with my left leg thrown over his legs. Lying beside him, I have a vision and laugh. I need to rest as much as I can because my mate is going to be taking me another five more times tonight. Finding everything I always dreamed of as a young pup. Feeling his love, safe and re-laxed, sleep takes me.

UNKNOWN

Sneaking into the dungeon, I see Stefanie chained in silver. She looks up to me. "Well, did you do what you were supposed to do?"

Taking the keys out of my pocket, I unlock the cell and walk in smiling at her. "I did what needed to be done."

"Well, take these silver chains off me so we can get out of here." She holds her wrists up to me. When I don't do as she asks, I can see she is getting pissed.

"I can't do that. The plan had to be altered. They still haven't noticed that their beloved daughter and nephew are missing. They will soon enough." I laugh like a mad scientist.

"What do you mean you altered it?" Stefanie starts to scream at me.

"Stop screaming! Lower your voice; someone will hear you." I tell her. "I waited 'til everyone left. I helped the pack members clean up. When the family left or went to bed, I created a distraction for Melina and Chase that took them down to the lake. No one would suspect me or my scent because they trust me. I quietly made my way into the kids' room while they were sleeping. I injected a small amount of wolfsbane into them. Wrapped them up in their blankets and put them into the back of my dodge pickup, then drove here for you."

"That's what we planned, so what has changed?" She looks at me confused.

"Well, I decided I am going to take you with me and leave you at the cabin that we set up to take those pups. It will look like you broke out of here and kidnapped them."

"Please don't do this. We are stronger together as a team." Sensing her fear.

"I can still help you." Pleading with me wasn't going to deter me from my new plan.

"You have a big mouth and I have no doubt you will sell me out to make yourself the hero." Making my way over to her, she throws her hands up to stop me. Stefanie can't move well being shackled, so I duck around her grab her by the neck she goes still. With my free hand, I pull the syringe out of my back pocket and inject it into her neck. Within seconds, she is unconscious. Unlocking her chains pick her up and throwing her into my truck with the pups and drive off.

Driving to the cabin on the western end of the packlands, I drop all three of them off and rush back because I want to be visible when they find out what all happen tonight. As I pass Colt's cabin, I see Melina sitting down by the lake, but Chase is gone. It's okay because they still don't have a clue. I make my way to my house. Needing to shower and burn my clothes. I can't afford to have any of their scents on me. After my shower, I sit outside watching my clothes burn, deciding how to proceed with the next step of my plan. Thinking back to the first day she came onto the packlands. Sitting back and watching her, I decided that day she would be my chosen mate. She is stunning and captivating. Colt and Zoey's mating ceremony was a great distraction. Neither of them have a clue that this was coming. Colt trusts me. Using the pups will make me look like a hero in his eyes. Stefanie will look like the villain she is, that is an added bonus. She doesn't know me, but she will soon I am going to have what is mine. Glancing up to the moon sparkling off the water, I smile. Be ready, my darling, I am coming to claim you as my mate. Even Chase won't stop me from making you all mine...Melina.